JOHN URBANCIK

CLOCKWORK RAVENS

JOHN URBANCIK
CLOCKWORK RAVENS

JOHN URBANCIK

CLOCKWORK RAVENS

for Morgan

1.

Rosa met the raven the day she arrived at the house.

It was a massive house at the top of a hill surrounded by rolling hills and woodland paths that, according to legend, ran all the way to Avalon. The house, with all its turrets and spires, was one of those structures that just kept building itself. New architectural features seemed to develop in all directions until the inside of the house was a kind of labyrinth.

Somewhere, there was a village where everyone knew about the house. But Rosa could not see the village from any window. She wandered the porch, sat for a while on the swing chair, tried to count the trees, the leaves in a given tree, the roses in the garden. She could count the statues. That was a more reasonable number. But they didn't immediately interest her. The roses, however, were so numerous, so overgrown, untended and practically wild within the confines of that garden, rose vines like ivy sprawling across the lattice–like gate. Strange, she thought, that a garden should require a gate when there was no fence.

Clouds gave the sky a texture like land in the light of the setting sun. Rosa walked through the roses, sniffed at the petals, even examined the thorns. She had never seen roses before, not in the ground, not growing. They were a delight. Some smelled so powerfully pungent, she thought she must have found a doorway to a fairy world. They shared her name, which had to mean something important, and the roses, that first day at least, seemed to come in every color: white, orange, pink, lavender, violet, and brilliant red.

Rosa was a child when she arrived at the house. At least, they told her she was a child. She was twelve, still startlingly small next to anyone else, and looked at everything as if it was the first time she'd ever seen it.

Which was likely true. She'd been sheltered. And the house, with all its grand promises of rich, even lucid experiences, also threatened to keep her sheltered from storms and from the world. It was true; she had never seen anything. She had never known anyone else. And she had never, until that first day at the house, seen anything so wondrous as those roses.

But she wasn't alone. Shiny black feathers, thick black beak, and eyes like coal, a raven hid among the roses. It startled her when she saw it. It didn't immediately fly away, so she leaned closer, careful not to get too close because that beak looked more dangerous than any thorn. The raven was magnificent and dignified, and it watched her with a dizzying eye, until she felt close to fainting.

"Oh, that can't be right," she said to no one and the raven. She straightened herself, shook her head of long white-blonde hair, and defied the raven, defied the oncoming storm, defied the garden itself. Inadvertently, she brushed a rose bush. One of the thorns bit her. She snatched her hand back to her chest. The raven fluttered and flew off into the night.

An immense drop of blood welled up on her finger. She thrust it into her mouth, sucking such a small amount of liquid, but not before a drop spilled onto her new white dress.

2.

The house was large and the land around it expansive, but the sky was grander, virtually endless, and that night covered by a thousand layers of smoky gray clouds. They seemed to twist and spin through the sky, woven by the gods themselves, though Rosa could not see the mountaintops they must call home.

At the supper table, under an enormous chandelier, with her mother and her uncles, no one seemed to notice the blood spot on her dress. It was near the hem, under the table, and could easily have been beets or wine, or even the strawberries served with desert.

She never knew if they saw her. Her uncles would discuss politics or textiles or opera or baseball, and they barely left room between breaths for her to even consider saying something. And what would she say? She had no experience with politics. She had never seen a baseball game or an opera. As to textiles – she had a thousand beautiful dresses, so maybe she might have an opinion, but they tended to talk about numbers, weights and volumes, square yards, shipping, and never about the color or texture or breath of a garment. She wasn't always certain they would know a garment if they saw it. They only wore suits, and boring gray suits at that, with the rare splash of color in a red necktie or handkerchief.

Only her mother ever addressed her directly. "Do your reading," she might say, or, "Wash your face." She would dab at Rosa's cheeks with a hot towel in the kitchen, would examine her disapprovingly if she got dirt on her shins. "Look at the state of your shoes. Those are leather, Rosa, darling. You really should take better care."

As she ate her strawberries, with cream and confectioner's sugar, a boisterous explosion of thunder signaled the clouds to let fall the rain. She threw down her spoon and ran out of the room. There were no windows in the dining room, just mirrors, glass, crystal, and thick oil paintings. The hallway to the front door seemed forever long, so she went through the kitchen and eventually out onto the back porch in time to see crazy arcs of lightning flick across the sky. The rain pummeled the earth. Wind bent the trees of the forest. The rose garden seemed to have drawn into itself, sheltering the more fragile buds with a canopy of marble statues and stronger petals. In the flashing lightning, shadows danced among the vines and bushes, and the statues seemed to move, to look back at her and smile.

Not all of those smiles were meant to be pleasant.

Rosa nearly fell back into the house.

But it was all a trick of the storm. The only thing real, other than the conflagration in the sky, other than the rolling and roiling thunder, other than the rain sneaking in under the awning of the porch to wet the bottom of her pretty dress, was the raven perched on the wood railing.

She wondered if it was the same bird.

It looked at her, examined her, read all of her secrets in an instant. Rosa didn't believe she had secrets outside of her dreams, but maybe the raven would find those, as well. Then the bird tapped its beak once on the wood and flew off without a sound. She – the raven – flew into the rain and wind and disappeared quickly in the murk.

She left something behind on the porch rail. Rosa got wetter when she went closer. It was a button, a black button dangling at the end of a few inches of string. It might have come from anywhere. It matched the raven's feathers. Even the string was black. She picked it up, held it toward the light and the lightning, trying to discern its meaning.

Her mother emerged from the house calling her name. Rosa stuffed the button into the little, virtually worthless pocket in her dress. "What do you think you're doing?"

"Isn't it beautiful?" Rosa said, gesturing toward the storm.

Briefly, as though it never really happened, her mother looked out over the garden and over the woods, into the velvet tapestry of sky over which the lightning was crackling. Rosa saw the electricity reflected in her mother's eyes. Her heart felt light for a moment. Her mother, who should have been beautiful but took efforts to not be, seemed about ready to believe in something again. Anything.

Instead, her mother tore her eyes from the spectacle and looked down at Rosa again. She wore her most common frown, the kind that suggested punishment was on its way. "You've ruined your dress. Look at this. Is that blood?"

She zeroed in on the single drop at Rosa's hem.

"No," Rosa said. "It must've been the wine."

Her mother seemed to consider this, seemed almost ready accept it. How else would you explain a single drop of blood on a dress when there were no obvious, and no hidden, wounds?

"Go to your rooms," mother said. "Clean yourself up. I don't want to see you again tonight. No dessert for you."

"I've already had dessert."

"No dessert tomorrow, then. Now get." She pointed back into the house, down the hall, and even up the stairs. "Not a word."

Rosa ran. Past her mother and into the house, down the long echoing hallway and up the wide, winding stairs. She ran until she reached her rooms, her bedroom and a private washroom with a claw foot tub, and slammed the door behind her. She wasn't scared. She was excited. Thrilled, even. From her windows, she could still see the storm in all its glory. And in her pocket, she'd managed to secret a gift from the raven into the house. A shiny black button on a thread. She wondered where it came from, if someone had lost the button from his shirt or if the owner was lost, wandering the woods – or dead and now merely a spirit.

She wondered what it was like for spirits wandering the woods after losing one of their buttons.

Maybe she could use it somehow. She had a needle and thread. She could sew it into one of her dresses. It would be purely decorative, of course. But it would be exciting. And it would be a garment of her own.

She washed her white dress that night, and took a bath herself, imagining she was floating down a river of rainwater through forests of roses and ivy, ravens flying overhead. She lingered in the bath so long, she pruned all her skin. What would the ravens think of her now?

In the dark of night, with the lights out, she began her secret sewing project. She added black thread of her own, and only stabbed herself with the needle once. It didn't make any more or less blood than the thorn. In the flickering of lightning, it looked like an eternal pool on the end of her finger. She pressed the blood into the cloth with the needle. It was a secret dress, one she didn't wear often, one that would hide in her closet until she needed it.

Lying in bed, she listened to the sounds of the storm, the screaming wind, the thunder as it grew more distant. She might have believed in banshees, then, had they been in the right country. But it was woodland outside, gardens but also forests, and the paths through those woods might very well lead to Ireland, to Eastern Europe, to distant Asian port cities like jewels on the other side of the world.

CLOCKWORK RAVENS

3.

Summer days passed as if in a dream. She explored parts of the house no one else seemed to use, discovering secret societies of spiders, sofas no one had ever sat upon, and a hidden doorway.

It was small, as if made for Rosa herself, and hidden behind a bureau that gleamed under its old world elegance and layers of dust. She saw the tracks of spiders and other insects along the top and side of the bureau, and on also the surface of the mirror attached to it. She stared at herself for a while because it made her look like someone else, someone older and sadder, and she didn't understand it. She almost told the mirror to keeps its opinions to itself.

She couldn't move the bureau. It was much too big and heavy for her. But she was small enough to squeeze in the space behind it, and that was all she needed to reach what was, essentially, half a door. Opening it inward, pushing forward, she discovered a house within the house.

She didn't think another house belonged inside her house. The room was similar to the one on the other side of the door, but dark and big and stuffed with shadows. There were sofas and tables and bookshelves, and a great big desk with a lamp. There was also a door. It stood ajar. Some light spilled into the room from that hallway. It was colder, in the house within a house, so she shivered and wrapped her arms around herself and tiptoed down the hall.

The light came from another room, its door wide open, where a man sat at a worktable. He wore funny glasses with appendages and a purple coat, and he worked with a series of strange tools on what must be a pocket watch. She'd never seen one up close. Its gold sparkled in the intense light aimed directly at it. The tools were long and slender, much like the man.

Quite suddenly, Rosa realized he had stopped working in the watch's guts and instead stared straight at her. "Oh, hi," she said. "I'm Rosa. I didn't know there was somebody already in the house."

His expression became quizzical. He responded, but the sounds he made were no words she knew. To be fair, she might recognize French and Spanish, but there were at least a dozen or a hundred more languages she couldn't even name, so he must've been speaking one of those. He didn't seem alarmed, so she stepped closer, to get a better look at what he was working on.

He smiled, but held out a hand and shook his head. He said something else. It was almost musical, the voice he spoke with and the language he used. She liked it immediately. She felt, then and there, this was a man who would listen to her, even if he couldn't understand her. Not like her uncles. He would protect her from the wolves in the night, even if there weren't wolves to be protected from; and he reminded her of her father, who was only a ghost lost on the other side of the world.

"Have you been here long?" she asked. "It feels like we've been here a long time. Why don't you ever dine with us? Are you one of those distant family my uncles never want to talk about?"

He said something, and gestured – kindly – back into the hall, back through the room and back through that door. Always, people wanted her to go somewhere other than where she was. Already, she was annoyed with it, and she wasn't even thirteen yet. She made a face, she stomped a foot, and said, "Okay, fine."

She turned like a soldier and marched out of the room, down the hall – it was like other halls in the house, but with thicker shadows and quieter floors – and back through the half door. She closed it behind her, but not so that she would make noise.

She raced downstairs and outside. She ran around the side of the house, looking for windows that must've belonged to the other house, but she couldn't be sure. She hadn't seen everything, and it took her ten minutes or more to run all the way around the house. She lost track, couldn't be sure of what she had or hadn't seen. She started counting the windows, but there were so many, and so many strange ones – little things hiding in corners and crevices – and a whole third floor to the house she hadn't even found a way to get to yet. Maybe the stairs to there were only in the *other* house. She would have to find a way.

She went around the house two and three times, counting and losing count of the windows, and eventually decided she would need to make a map. A sketch. Something to track the windows so she could know.

As she passed the rose garden, the raven called to her.

It was a single caw, a common enough sound, but it almost sounded like the raven said her name. *Rosa*, as if it had contained two syllables. The raven perched on the arm of one of the marble goddesses. The statues in the rose garden weren't full size, so the goddess was not even as tall as Rosa.

"Are you sure?" she asked the raven. It was the same raven. She'd been back several times. But this was second time she brought a gift.

Under the raven's clawed feet, Rosa found an earring. Only

one, not a pair. The clasp had been damaged, but it might be real gold. The jewels, however, were likely fake: a series of shimmery things resembling diamonds, five of them in an arc, none very large. Rosa didn't have diamond earrings of her own. She liked the way it caught and refracted the sunlight. It was almost like looking into the heart of a rainbow.

The raven hopped a step back so Rosa could pick up the earring. The end was sharp, where it was broken, and the trace of blood was still wet.

"Did you steal this from someone's ear?" she asked.

The raven regarded her a moment, then opened its mouth as if to speak. Of course, no words came out, no sound at all, but it wouldn't have surprised Rosa to hear it say, "Nevermore." She'd found a book in the library and read a little about ravens. She knew what they meant. This one must've been an emissary of her father, and probably it should have been speaking to Rosa's mother instead of her.

Mistake or not, the raven had come to her, and she adored it. "Thank you so much," she said. "Do you have a name?"

Again, the raven said nothing.

"I might call you Lenore, if that's okay," Rosa said. "I know it's not quite right, but it's not entirely wrong, is it?"

The raven seemed to nod her head. Or not. Then she took off, flying away from the garden and away from the house, into the thick woods Rosa still had not really explored.

4.

The woods were scary thick and lush. The sounds that came from them were indescribable, rustlings unlike anything in Rosa's experience. As the summer waned, and her uncles turned their attention to business, Rosa and her mother were left alone in the house more often. As big as the house was, it was easy to get lost inside, or separated, sometimes for hours and sometimes for days. Taking advantage of this, in the earliest light of dawn, when the sun was merely an idea and a fiery line of red laid upon the eastern horizon, Rosa snuck out of the house, past the gardens, and crept into the forest.

She knew there were would be lions, tigers, bears, that sort of thing; but she wasn't afraid. She didn't know if she could ever be afraid of anything. She didn't want to get caught before her adventure, though, so she left when the light was thin and shadows swept across the land. She wore her special dress, the one with the button and the earring sewn into the lining. Those would protect her, and the thread itself should lead her back home if she got lost.

The forest wall was a line of trees, imposing and impassable trunks twice as thick around as she was. Where there were breaks between the trunks, there were prickly bushes, brambles overrun with thorns and the occasional wild roses. From the house, she had seen paths, and she was small, so Rosa was determined to find a way in before her mother stepped out onto the porch with coffee and, in the opening light of the day, saw her out there. She was small, so she didn't need a path so much as the slightest crack. When she found it, she crawled under the brambles, only briefly catching but not tearing her dress. Then she was inside the forest.

The light was different on the other side. It filtered through the leaves, above and toward the east, making everything seemed greener and yellower, more heavily saturated than it should be. There were birds, and on the sides of the trees moss like rugs of emeralds, and narrow paths carved perhaps by deer or the wolves that stalked them.

She tied a piece of string to one of the trees to remind her of the way back. She might not really want to go back, but when dusk approached she probably wouldn't have a choice. Nocturnal creatures in the forest would eat her up, just like in the fairy tales. She was small, but still a tasty morsel, of that she was sure.

Her mother had told her the woods would be dirty, full of foul beasts and their stenches, dangerous in too many ways to count. With every step deeper into the forest, Rosa believed this less. Yes, spider's webs in the trees captured some of the sunlight that should have filtered down to her level. Yes, there were odors and aromas she had never smelled. But they were rich, earthy, far more real than what she had inside the house's polished wood, dust, and stagnation.

And the dirt wasn't dirty at all. It was comfortable. She left her shoes at the base of the tree with the string. She wanted to feel the dirt and the roots and the moss on her bare feet.

More than once, she heard movement in the leafy canopy above her, but she only ever caught the briefest glimpse of birds or squirrels or chipmunks. She knew now the woods were definitely a fairy wood, belonging to otherworldly creatures, so she shouldn't trust everything she saw. She wouldn't. She was smarter than that. Her mother, after all, had raised her well, hadn't she?

Rosa walked for a while, then ran, arms extended and head held high, breathing deeply of the woody aromas, falling in love with the hyper-intensive light and the way it made everything seem stronger, sharper, more real.

She hadn't thought to pack anything for lunch, and had skipped breakfast, so it wasn't long before she was hungry. She didn't know what she could eat in the woods. Berries, if she'd found any, might be poisonous. Mushrooms might make her grow, and that would be awful because she wouldn't fit any of her clothes any more. Her mother already complained when she needed new dresses every season, that she grew too fast as it was. Rosa never felt any bigger, but she must be.

She found a break in the woods, like a copse of treelessness, where the sunrays fell in their full power. Some of the trees had fallen, had blackened; the trees growing there were thinner than all the rest of the forest, and there weren't as many. She danced in the fallen leaves, brown and crunchy and out of season. She didn't wonder long about what had happened there. She danced as though the forest belonged to her, as though she was one of the fairy folk, as though all the trees and woodland creatures danced with her.

She danced until she was out of breath, then laid down in a shaft of sunlight, against the moss on one side of the trees. She marveled at the softness of it, the dewiness despite how late in the day it must be, and the heat in that light.

Rosa dreamt of falling asleep. Daydreams were different than night dreams. When she wasn't asleep, she had more control over what happened to her. She didn't have to run from wicked evil creatures with sickly brown skin or hide from the things with eyes. She could dream of princes, princesses, horses running wild through the woods, and ravens sneaking into the house through windows she hadn't yet mapped.

There were so many windows, hundreds and maybe thousands of them, some not much bigger than her head, and others, like in the grand living room, floor to ceiling. She'd had to mark windows inside with pieces of tape so when she was outside, she could indicate in her little book which windows belonged to which rooms. Empty bedroom. Empty bedroom. Unused bath. Library.

She didn't know what to name every room. But she couldn't map all the windows. Some rooms that seemed adjacent from the inside, whose windows should have been next to each other, were separated by other panes of glass that never revealed any lights from inside.

She was convinced the ravens lived inside the house, so of course she dreamt of them living in all the places her mother wouldn't allow her to go. Not that her mother forbade her; inside the house, Rosa seemed to be free to explore. But there were places she couldn't reach, or couldn't find again. When she asked about them, her mother told her to stop pretending, eat your soup, don't make me send you to bed without supper again.

She couldn't ask her uncles.

In that copse of sunlight in the woods, without sleeping, she dreamt of statues in the rose garden coming to life, having tea, throwing a parade. She asked those little goddesses and goat men what they wanted in life, why they'd been made, if they missed their homelands. They merely laughed, threw garlands of rose petals, and drank wine.

They couldn't give her answers she didn't already know, not even in her own dreams.

But she was hungry, so she had to go back. She retraced her

steps as well as she could. The paths in the woods were numerous, once she could see them, and crisscrossed frequently. She couldn't trust the angles of sunlight because the sun moved during the day. It wasn't something she could count on.

She found a small graveyard.

A dozen stones stood in two uneven rows. Names had been carved into them, but not names she recognized, not even letters she recognized. They must be from the language spoken by the watchmaker inside. She didn't know, couldn't be sure, and she hadn't brought anything to copy the words onto.

She tried to sound them out anyway. But how did you pronounce letters from the other side of the world? Her mouth didn't work that way. Neither did her eyes.

The stones were nearly the color of the forest. The granite had been overrun by lichen and moss; she'd almost missed them entirely. She tied another piece of string to a tree, eye height, so she might find them again, then headed back in the direction she believed she had come. The sun was too directly above her to be certain anymore. Paths twisted in different directions now. Her legs started to ache. Her stomach rumbled. She wasn't afraid of getting lost in the woods. The fey might take her to their secret fairy villages and make her queen for a night, feed her ice cream and shortcakes, and break out a band of fairy flutes and violins. Or they might throw her in a dungeon and leave her in the dark.

If she came home after dark, her mother would do the same.

Finally, far off in one direction that wasn't straight ahead of her, she saw her first string. She had to fight against the forest to get there, no longer following a path but climbing through stickers and over fallen tree limbs. It wasn't that the woods didn't want her to leave, but they weren't going to make it easy. She had to want to escape, and prove it, even if she didn't know if she believed it.

She reached her string, left it there, then crawled out through the forest wall. The field seemed larger than ever before, and the house smaller because it was so far away. As she walked, clouds drifted through the sky, wind drifted through the fields, and dragonflies flitted here and there.

From this angle, from so far away, the house looked different: darker, with odder angles, gables where they maybe shouldn't have been. What if it wasn't the same house?

But it was the same rose garden. When she got there, though, she noticed a fresh row of blossoms, crimsons instead of reds, paler yellows, pinks tinged with violets, and some so dark they were indigo.

The house was the same house. Maybe Rosa's adventure in the forest had changed her so that she looked on it with new eyes. She was still young. She understood, at least intellectually, that there was more growth ahead of her.

Numerous doors led into the house. She hadn't opened all of them, or found them all from the inside, but this one she'd never noticed before. It was hidden in a kind of alcove that was really just a strange angle in the house. It didn't face the rose garden, but it opened in that direction. The watchmaker emerged from the door carrying a basket of gardening tools and wearing his purple coat. He shielded his eyes against the sun. It wasn't quite twilight yet, but Rosa had been out for most of the day.

The man was whistling. But he stopped when he saw Rosa staring at him.

He squinted, and even rubbed his eyes, and asked something in his own language. She didn't understand it, but the individual letters sounded like they belonged on the stones she had seen. "I live here, too," she said, pointing toward her bedroom window. It was around the other side of the house, not facing the rose garden, but when he turned to look, she was sure he knew which room she meant. He said something else, shrugged, then beckoned her to follow him into the rose garden.

He walked among them with intention and purpose, not like she ever did. And he wandered, taking time to examine specific blooms, sniffing some and sometimes motioning for her to do the same. Finally, he reached a rose so darkly indigo it was really black. He shook his head and muttered some sort of curse, which she would later practice trying to say in the dark of her room. With a snip of the pruning shears, he cut it off at its lowest point.

He didn't show it to her, but crushed the head of the rose in his hand. He explained why, in his language, in a way she almost comprehended, then dropped the crumpled petals into his basket.

He looked at her, said something, shook the basket with the dead rose petals and other cutting tools, then nodded toward the house, toward one of the doors she'd always known.

She understood that much. She left the man in the garden. He went about his work, ignoring her now, and she entered the house through the big twin front doors.

Her mother stood there, one hand on a hip thrown sharply to one side. "Where have you been?" she asked first, then, "What have you done? Look at the state of you." She knelt in front of Rosa, rubbed at her cheeks as if trying to clean them of something she couldn't even see. "And look at your pretty little dress. Oh, will you ever learn, Rosa? *Ever?*"

Her mother stood again abruptly. "Go to your rooms. No supper, no dessert, nothing. Clean yourself, you're a mess, I don't want to see you looking like this again, not tonight and not ever. Clean yourself, and clean your dress, and mend it." She was shaking her head in disbelief.

Rosa raced upstairs to her room. She closed and locked the door. She knew mother had the second key, but she'd at least get a warning of that key in the keyhole. The lock was loud, and not always easy to convince. She wanted to get out of her dress and rip it to shreds, but this was her special dress, with the button and the earring, the gifts of the raven, and she wasn't about to destroy it.

Sure, it was dirty, but not exactly ruined. Two little rips in the lacy fabric were easy to fix. She reworked part of the hem. With her thread and needle, she only cut herself twice – the first time accidentally, but then she stabbed the corresponding finger on the other hand so she could watch them both bleed. They were just twin drops of blood, almost inky in the dying light. She smooshed them together, smearing the blood redly on her fingers but not really changing anything. The pain was subtle, hardly anything at all. She saw maps in the bloodstains that might lead her away from this house, to distant lands like Prague and Perth, Pretoria and Paris; she saw hints of the grid-like paths of the rose garden and also of the forest. She saw insinuations of rooms within her own home, where perhaps the watchmaker lived.

Ultimately, she saw nothing in her blood but twin blotches. She ran a bath with hot water, submerged, and scrubbed herself clean. There was nothing else to do. She took the needle with her. When she was done, she stayed in the tub to watch the water spin down the drain. She pricked her finger again. Maybe it hurt more when she didn't mean to do it. She squeezed two, three drops of blood into the tub to watch the red spiral into the water and snake down the drain. When the water was gone, all of it but the dregs, she had to open up the spigot again to clear the traces of blood. She didn't want her mother finding those.

As she toweled dry, she saw the raven at her bedroom window. The window was open, but the bird hadn't come into the room. Instead, it had sat there and watched her in the bath. Seen, discovered in its spying, the raven made a series of clicking sounds as it flew off.

The raven left another gift: a thimble. Gold or copper or brass, it had a vine and leaf carefully etched into it. In places, especially along the edges of the etching, it had gone green. It smelled like pennies, but also like the forest, as though it had been buried for years. Dirt was caked onto it, especially inside, where she would put her finger.

She smiled. The raven didn't want her to hurt herself.

Rosa took the thimble to the big sink in her big bathroom and washed it thoroughly. It bled coppery dirt under the water. She felt the needle pricks in her fingers as she washed it, but that was fine. The pain reminded her of the love of the raven, of the importance of its gifts and promises, and that there would, one day, be a way of escaping this big house.

She stored the thimble with her needle and thread. She watched out the window as the last of the daylight disappeared. She didn't hear her mother and uncles at the dining table, but she smelled roast meats and vegetables, and she could easily imagine the intricacies of the crystal glasses holding wine. She suspected they laughed at Rosa and her misfortunes and her stupid little dreams. Her stomach rumbled with hunger. She'd eaten nothing all day. She poured a big glass of water, but that really did nothing for her stomach. She tried to sleep listening to the thunder inside her. She tried but couldn't. She kept seeing the graveyard, the black rose being cut and crumpled, the raven and the thimble.

Someone knocked, gently, on her bedroom door. Three

times. Three little knocks that sounded nothing like her mother, who would pound on the door if she wanted to announce herself – or merely unlock it. Three timid knocks, almost like the sound a raven would make. Tentatively, wrapped in her best robe, Rosa tiptoed to the door and tried to look out through the keyhole. In stories, everyone seemed able to see through keyholes, and the things they saw were sometimes mysterious and sometimes illicit. But they were always looking into rooms, and here she was trying to look out of the room to see someone or something in the hallway. She saw nothing.

She unlocked the door and pulled it open just a few inches. There was a small tray on the floor, a silver tray, with a small glass of wine – a thimbleful, she thought – and an assortment of berries, thin slices of sausage, and a few pieces of bread. It wasn't a feast. And while it certainly hadn't been brought by her mother, whoever had left it there had disappeared after knocking.

Maybe he watched from a shadow, or through the keyhole of another door. Maybe he perched in a crevice in the ceiling where he could watch her unseen. None of her uncles would have brought her food; they never seemed to notice she was there. It must've been the watchmaker.

The telltale sign: a single black rose petal.

5.

As summer began to cool, Rosa's birthday approached. Her mother often made a big deal of this, sometimes even making a cake, often playing special records that she kept hidden from everyday use. "Some songs," her mother had said, "can only be enjoyed because of the scarcity."

In fact, all songs were scarce. Her mother rarely allowed Rosa to use the record player, and she had no such thing in her rooms. She wondered what it might be like to play an instrument, to blow through a silver rod and make flute sounds, to strum strings, to beat on a drum. Her mother, however, said noise of any sort was rarely acceptable.

Just those two times every year: once for her mother's spring birthday, once for hers in the autumn. As the day approached, Rosa went out less, wanting to steer clear of doing anything that might upset her mother.

The day before her birthday, Rosa couldn't get out of bed. She felt sick to her stomach. Her whole body felt heavy. Her skin felt too tight and ill-fitting. A headache formed by midday and only worsened. She got up several times to fill her water glass, but otherwise stayed in bed. Pain, starting in the small of her back, spread like little pebbles through her veins.

No one seemed to notice.

She couldn't sleep, couldn't focus on her books, and quickly lost interest in the shapes of the clouds, even if those shapes did include a dragon.

She felt weak, dizzy, and nauseous, and she barely slept through the night. The morning of her birthday, her mother knocked on the door and let herself in. "What do you think you're doing?"

"I don't feel well."

Her mother came to the bed, sat on the side of it, and put her hand on Rosa's forehead. "You don't seem to have a fever."

"I can't move my legs."

"Nonsense." Her mother snapped to her feet and added, "We'll have your birthday breakfast. Get dressed and come downstairs." The way she said it, *immediately* was implied and unnecessary to add. She left the room, closing the door behind her, leaving Rosa to crawl out of the big bed and make her way to her closet. Her mother would want her to wear the fancy white dress with the ribbons. A special day required a special outfit.

She splashed her face at the sink, but it didn't make her feel any better. She dressed slowly, without enthusiasm, struggling to lift her arms enough to get them into the dress. She took an extra moment to glance out the window. Her birthday looked cold outside, though it was only cooler than it had been. The sun seemed only barely able to pierce a mist that covered the entire world. Maybe that was why she felt so terribly; she hadn't been getting enough essential sunlight. She feared it might be even worse during the winter.

She clung to the banister as she descended the stairs. In the dining room, her uncles had gathered in several distinct groups. They looked as ashen as she felt. Her mother was the only source of vibrant color in her new yellow sundress. Special occasions called for special outfits.

Breakfast was spread across the table: pancakes and biscuits, bacon and sausage, heaping piles of blueberries and strawberries, even a tall glass of fresh chocolate milk. The smells of all these things coalesced into a thick soupy odor that went straight to Rosa's head.

One of her uncles looked in her direction and smiled. It was so rare a thing it startled her. She never realized how toothy her uncles' smiles could be. But it was brief, as if for a moment he'd forgotten he was supposed to ignore her. He went back to the conversation about commodities and commerce. The words they used were dreadfully dusty and archaic.

She looked again at the breakfast spread. The good china had been set out, and the silver had been polished – no, Rosa herself had polished it just a week ago, and it hadn't been used since.

Her mother stood over the whole thing with her arms crossed and her eyes steady. She wore nothing like a smile. Indeed, she seemed to be losing all her good spirits in a slow leak that collapsed her lips and narrowed her eyes.

"What?" her mother asked, enunciating every word as its own sentence, "Have? You? Done?"

Rosa had done a great many things. She had sought the house's basement and only found crawlspaces. She had failed to find her way back into the other house within the house, but she had tried numerous times. She had taken a book from a library. It was still in her room. She had listened to the thunderstorms, run through the rose garden, cut herself more than once climbing the stone statues in the yard.

But she couldn't think of any one thing her mother wanted to know about now. She tried, but nothing came to her. She hadn't run far enough in any direction to find the nearest village. She hadn't climbed onto the roof, though she'd found a place where she might. She hadn't broken any windows or lamps or vases. Nothing.

She drew a blank, and her mother seemed intent on an answer.

A flush of weakness washed over Rosa. Her knees buckled, but she did not fall. She felt a faint building inside her, like what happened to women in all those old books her mother probably wouldn't approve of her reading – maybe that's what she wanted to know? – but she refused to let it take hold. Her fingers tingled with ice, her eyes felt cold and dry, her tongue stuck to the roof of her mouth. She squeezed one hand into a fist, a small and incapable fist, without power or presence, but it was the only way to be sure she still had fingers at the end of it. Her stomach, absorbing all the odors of a breakfast she realized she would never eat, tried to turn over inside her.

"You're bleeding," her mother said.

Rosa hadn't cut herself. There were no wounds on her fingers or her hands. She couldn't see her own face, but surely she would have felt if she'd scraped or scratched it against something. But her mother was looking down, so Rosa lowered her eyes and saw the spot of blood at the center of her white dress.

"Oh," she said, because she didn't know what else to say. It was her best dress. Her mother would kill her, if the wound didn't kill her first. One of her uncles snuffed haughtily.

Her mother shook her head and pointed out of the dining room, back down the hall and up the stairs and all the way to Rosa's room. "Get out of here," she said, "and clean yourself up. I can *not* believe you came down here in that condition."

Rosa wanted to run from the room, to flee and retreat, but her legs lacked the strength. Instead, she swayed, tumbled sideways, and fell to the floor, banging her knee and elbow, igniting pains in her back and abdomen and thighs. Tears fell from her eyes, but she refused to cry aloud, not in front of her uncles and certainly not in front of her mother. She didn't sob, didn't fall apart, simply tried to crawl out of the dining room as quickly as she could.

This aroused the uncles' attention. Now, for perhaps the first time, they fell silent. They watched her crawl. They watched, making no move to help or comfort her, as Rosa dragged herself into the hallway. She couldn't make her legs work properly. She felt dizzy. The hall tilted in two or three directions simultaneously.

Behind her, her mother sat at the dining table. Rosa heard the knife and fork clacking against the fancy plate as her mother ate. Rosa crawled far enough away not to be seen, then curled against the side of the hall to catch her breath. The pain receded, though she knew it would come back. When she felt able, she pulled herself to her feet, then used the wall for support as she walked to the stairs. She took a deep breath before attempting the climb. She made it halfway before a surge of abdominal pain almost crumpled her to her knees. She clung to the banister until it passed, then completed the climb. Her room seemed to be a thousand miles away. On either side of her, hallways opened up into other sections of the house she had never seen or imagined. Others of her uncles – she never knew how many there were, they seemed all interchangeable, faceless and nameless – ceased their conversations to follow her progress.

Finally reaching her room, she slammed the door behind her and locked it and fell to the ground to breathe deeply and heavily for a while. She looked down at her dress, the sunburst of red at the center of it. For a while, the pain was unbearable, so she sat there and watched the blood slowly spreading and didn't do anything else. Eventually, she got back to her feet, and she got out of the dress. She put it in the bathtub. She would have to clean it. She didn't know how to clean up that much blood. She hadn't expected to have so much inside her. She'd only ever seen a drop at a time before. The drops had been so very pretty.

She ran water into the tub, but left it for tomorrow. Or the next day. She had no idea how long she'd be sick. She wondered if she'd die. Would the raven come to guide the ghost of her to heaven?

Rosa glanced at her bedroom window. There she was: the raven, her brilliant black feathers, her sharp little eye and thick rough beak. The raven watched without judgement, unlike her uncles who had seemed, for the first time, concerned – though maybe not in a good way. Not concerned, but interested.

The raven flew away, out into the daylight, but she'd left a birthday present. It must be something special. Rosa had a birthday only once a year. Even ravens must be aware of their significance. The gift glimmered in the sunlight. But when Rosa picked it up and examined it, turning it over and over, running her thumb along the sharp edges and smooth side, she read the words over and over again. It was a bottle cap, slightly bent, and though it was yellow, it said *Orange Crush*, it said *Carbonated Beverage*, and it said *Color Artificial*.

Rosa spent most of the rest of the day in bed. Twice, she refilled her water glass. She felt a little better by twilight. She ate a chocolate from the stash she'd started keeping hidden in her closet, and she took a bath. She stayed in bed the next morning, and in the afternoon felt well enough to clean her sheets and dress, which was enough to exhaust her.

Her mother never came to check on her. Her mother never asked what was wrong. One time, her mother paused outside Rosa's door, stopped maybe to listen, but she didn't knock, didn't use her key, and didn't come in.

CLOCKWORK RAVENS

6.

Some days later, after Rosa had finally eaten, when she had regained her strength and sewed the bottle cap into her special dress, she sat in the rose garden absorbing the sunlight and the fragrances. Different roses smelled differently, which she had never expected, some fruitier, some earthier, some richer, and some so delicate she was afraid she might break the fragile scents just be breathing them in.

At one point, the raven watched her from atop one of the little goddess statues. She made no sound. When Rosa looked directly at her, she flew off, only to return a few minutes later to take another perch.

Rosa looked at the house, comparing all the windows to those on the map she'd sketched in a notepad. There were additional windows today, or she had missed them when she'd initially been drawing. She counted thirteen, at least, but she kept losing count because the sun's rays would get especially intense or an unidentifiable sound would echo from the woods.

After a particular sound came three or four times, she turned her attention to the line of trees. It looked like a distant army getting ready to march against the house, her mother and her uncles, and even herself. It seemed unfriendly, the way the light struck the trees, the way the shadows swayed in anticipation. Then she heard the sound again, a single snap, and the whole of the forest seemed to shudder. The raven answered with a low, agitated caw.

"I don't know what it is," she told the raven.

There weren't many clouds in the sky, so it couldn't be thunder unless it was very far away, but it sounded more like cracks than booms. It sounded manmade. Unnatural. Did they have woodsmen here? She had never seen one. The uncles, in their prim and perfect gray suits, with their spectacles and cigarettes and the overly precise syllables in all of their words, could never have been woodsmen. They wouldn't know how to use an axe, wouldn't know the shape of one, wouldn't know the sound of it cutting the air.

She didn't know that sound, either.

The crack came again. It had to be an axe. A sharp one. If it had been swung against her flesh, it would hurt, and she'd likely never forget the pain for as long as she lived. The trees must feel the same. She watched them tremble. "Oh my," she said, in sympathy, in surprise, in fear. What if the woodsman made his way through the woods following the strings she had left to guide him to her? What if the wolves didn't protect her?

It was the middle of the day. The sun was bright, the air hot as though summer had come again. She should have been counting the swings of that axe. She thought she could do that, she could swing an axe to protect herself, but she didn't know if she could be so brutal as to chop down a tree without cause. Surely the woodsman had a reason.

The sound didn't come again. Eventually, the forest seemed to relax: the trees swayed gently again in the breeze, and the normal sounds of cicadas and crickets slowly returned. She hadn't even realized they'd gone silent.

Rosa returned to the house. To the windows. There seemed now to only be as many as she'd drawn on her map. The locations of some remained a mystery. She'd been outside long enough. She went in to search for the inside corners of the house.

The halls twisted and turned quite frequently. They always led her places she didn't want to go, and never allowed her to reach the corners, the turrets, the spires. Maybe these belonged exclusively to the other house inside, but she hadn't been able to find that, either. When she turned a corner, she came upon one of the uncles standing straight, not unlike a tree, reading a book he'd pulled from a hallway shelf. He glanced at her, which was more than any of the uncles had ever done before, and returned to his book.

Another hall led to a room with mirrors. It wasn't grand or overwhelming, but each wall carried a larger rectangular mirror. They seemed to be tinted in different hues: blue, green, yellow, and red. The colors were subtle, almost nonexistent, but each transformed her reflection into something else. She looked cold in the blue mirror, frozen, as if trapped in the teeth of winter. The green mirror made her look vibrant and delicious, like fresh meat awaiting the kill. In the yellow, she looked warm, even hot, overcome with deliria and mania and fever visions she couldn't even describe. The red mirror made her look dangerous. She liked that one best. She flexed her teeth when she smiled into it, then scowled, then laughed. She could hardly maintain the illusion. But when she laughed, her own noise masked another, a growl like a wolf's, that seemed to originate from somewhere in the room itself.

But there was no furniture to hide behind. All the walls seemed solid. No windows opened up to the outside. She couldn't hear it anymore. Maybe it had followed her from the yellow mirror. She didn't know the properties of mirrors. Maybe the library had a book that would enlighten her, but her wanderings – no, her quests for corners and other secrets – never led her to such a place. A smoking room with racks of bourbon and brandy and cigars. A small dining room, cozy and meant for two, with dark lush wood and velvet. A billiard room where the table seemed fragile like porcelain. It was intricately carved, and the balls gleamed like little skulls. They hadn't been used in so long, dust had settled on them, and spiders had left their webs to dry. She picked up the cue ball. It was cold, smooth but also rough, as though the roughness had been so well achieved it looked and felt glassy until she gave it her full attention. She dropped it on the table, relieved when it didn't roll against any of the others and echo the cracking sound of earlier. She didn't really run from the room, but she did.

Upstairs, there were a row of bedrooms that clearly belonged to the uncles. They were as neutral in color as the uncles, as though all vibrancy had been drained from even the rugs and chandeliers. This might be where they slept. She honestly didn't know. She'd never seen the uncles retire for bed or rise in the morning.

She walked in on one of the uncles. He sat at a writing desk, though he didn't appear to be writing anything. He was staring out the window, so deep in thought he hadn't heard her open the door.

"Uncle," she said.

With excruciating deliberation, he turned his gaunt face toward her. She rarely saw only one of the uncles at a time. His cheeks were pale and hollow and sunken. His eyes were dark, highlighted by rings underneath. His hair was wispy but carefully manicured and arranged. His necktie was as gray a red as she'd ever seen. Even with his suit he seemed thin, insubstantial, hardly real at all. Looking at Rosa, he smiled. He leaned forward, though he didn't move from the desk.

He looked hungry when he grinned.

She ran from his bedroom, closing the door, and hid in an alcove in the hall. She waited for him to come out and chase after her. She was sure it would happen, but it didn't. After a long while, she decided to breathe again, a full intake of air rather than the shallow and quiet things she'd been attempting.

Usually, the uncles seemed preoccupied with themselves. They never even noticed her. All together in a pack, they seemed harmless and innocuous. But the one by himself, turning all his attention on her, exuded menace and ill-intent, all in the way he looked and loomed. He hadn't really moved, hadn't made any kind of threat, hadn't even said hello – but maybe the silence contributed. Did the uncles even know her name? Could they see the color of her hair, so white it almost echoed their pallor?

She didn't want to resemble the uncles.

After that, she found the music room.

It was a big room with a shining piano at the center of it. Someone had cared for the instrument. Not a fleck of dust could be found, neither on the piano itself nor the two big windows nor in the shafts of sunlight bursting through them.

She looked outside. She was on the other side of the house, away from the rose garden, looking out on the vegetables, the long winding dirt road, and a stretch of fields descending the hills and leading to more woods.

The piano was open. Its top was open, its keys were open, and it practically begged to be played. Certainly her mother had never seen this instrument. She would've locked it up tight and covered it with white sheets or maybe even smashed it to bits with an axe. Rosa could imagine the painful wails of the piano as its strings were cleaved and its keys were smashed and its life stolen.

She ran her fingers across the ivory keys. Lightly, so as not to press them, so as not to attempt to make music. She wouldn't know how. Some of the records her mother had played for birthdays in the past had included pianos, but she'd never actually imagined she might touch one and play one and make music of her own.

She pressed a key near the far left side. It resounded deeply and loudly. No doubt, the noise of it echoed through the halls, into bedrooms and studies and libraries, down the stairs and into kitchens and parlors, finally into the ears of her mother. Rosa snatched her hand away. The note continued to vibrate, diminishing far more slowly than she would have hoped. Maybe it was only in her head. That might be a blessing.

Rosa listened for any reaction. Next time, at least, if there ever was to be a next time, she'd shut the music room door and not risk summoning demons and monsters and mothers alike.

At first, it seemed like she would be spared having to answer for such insolence. She stood breathlessly next to the piano when she heard footsteps in the hall. They were too heavy to be the uncles; they walked with too much stealth, like whispers and mists. Her mother would walk more swiftly, with grim determination, and burst into the room like a conflagration.

The watchmaker stepped into the room. He smiled when he saw her. He said hello – in his language, but what else would he have said? He entered the room. He gave her a little bow, nothing fancy, sat at the piano, and raised his hands. His long, spindly fingers wriggled. Then he dropped them on the keys and made them dance.

As his fingers danced, the piano sang.

She didn't know the song, but she knew it was a minor key because of the way it made her feel. At first, she was excited to listen, thrilled at the sound, but as he played the music seemed to darken her soul and her mood. Outside, clouds drifted in front of the sun, obscuring it, adding melancholy to the whole of the world, and soon it was softly raining.

But the rain didn't stop him from playing. Rosa stood there, still as a statue, enraptured, entrapped, unable to flee if she wanted to.

He swayed as his fingers danced. He played with his eyes closed. The piano seemed to respond to his thoughts more than his fingers, the notes preceding him and mourning for him. The song reminded her of her father, whom she had hardly known, but also of the mother she had never known, the echo of who she might have been, the memories of who she would never become.

The song also reminded Rosa of herself, younger and older than she was now, more naïve and childlike, more mature and dying, as though by capturing the ends of her, the melody had enveloped all of her.

Rosa trembled.

The watchmaker finished with a trickle of low chords, left his fingers lingering on the notes to let them stretch toward infinity. At some point, he turned to look at her, and he smiled. It wasn't like the uncle's smile. It was softer, warmer, and maybe a bit more frightening.

"Thank you," Rosa said quickly before running out of the room.

CLOCKWORK RAVENS

7.

The music haunted her. It stayed with her, followed her down the hall even when the watchmaker wasn't playing, crept through her head, infected her bones. She ran to her room and hid under her covers, but there was no hiding from the sounds – and the way they made her feel. Alive and dead. Fascinated and afraid. Complete and empty.

She considered jumping out her window. It wasn't a long way down. She probably wouldn't do anything more than hurt herself. The raven would most definitely not approve. She saw it now looking up at her from the rose garden. The bird didn't seem to care about the rain, which was gentle and soothing and sounded like the music.

The music followed her into the tub and under the water. It lingered over supper. It drifted between images in her dreams even when she didn't remember them. The single song had sounded so much more resonant, so much more alive, than anything her mother had ever found on records for their birthdays. No wonder her mother didn't enjoy music. She'd never really heard it. The tinny, weak, distant sounds of those recordings paled compared to the real thing.

For days and even weeks, Rosa could recall every note of the song, every high and low, every chord and triad, every shift in the melody, every movement of the story it told.

She didn't know the story, but it felt like hers. Not that it belonged to her, but that it was the story of and about her. It told her past and her future. It revealed all her secrets, but she wasn't ready for those to be revealed. She didn't think she needed to know them herself yet.

The song followed her into the rose garden. She was only able to get away from it when she went back into the woods.

She found her way in easily, like her body remembered the steps she'd taken. She crawled through the underbrush and found the string she'd tied to a trunk just a few paces away. She hadn't snuck out before dawn this time. Her mother seemed more and more distant, so she'd simply walked, though she went out through a door facing the rose garden rather than the back. She didn't want to make it obvious.

Though the brush had been still green, inside the forest was an explosion of yellows and reds. The leaves above her had all changed color, so the sunlight filtering through the canopy seemed to rain gold over her. Even the moss seemed to have gone to gold, reflecting the new colors of the forest.

She carefully picked her way back to the graveyard. It was a long walk, and not straight, but she found her way without incident. Seven stones in one row, five in another, names and dates engraved unevenly. They were old. The earth had begun to reclaim them. The tops of the stones felt like they had once been rough but time had smoothed them and coated them with thin layers of moss.

In the months since she'd first found the stones, she still hadn't learned to read the names. Rosa sat in the middle of them and acknowledged each individually, doing her best with the letters. Maybe these belonged to the people who had first lived in the house. Did that make them distant relatives? Ancestors? She didn't know how that worked. The uncles never talked about such things.

She stayed with the stones so long, it started to snow. The first snow of the season, it must've been early. They were tiny drifting flakes, and only a few made it through the leaves above her, but the colors had still been so vibrant. They couldn't possibly have reached winter already.

Eventually, she realized the vibrant golds had been replaced by crisp browns, and a layer of dead, crackling leaves had preceded the snow. She'd been visiting the graves every day for weeks, and the days had all run together. There had been meals, and uncles lurking in the hallways, and her mother telling her to sit straight and not slurp and to stop ruining her dresses.

She had been stopping in the rose garden, pulling blooms of the right colors, primarily red but also pink and black. She'd started keeping the roses in a wood box she had found. It had once carried cigars, so the smell was pungent and enticing, and it kept the roses dry. She sprinkled a few crushed petals over the stones, an offering of sorts, and said, "I might not be back much now that winter is here, but I know where you are and you know where I am, and everything will be good like in stories."

The graves did not respond. The dried leaves left residue on her fingers.

Returning through the woods, watched perhaps by deer and wolves and rodents and birds, Rosa found the field had been coated in white. The house had been blanketed. Everything looks enormously peaceful and quiet and lifeless. She caught snowflakes on her tongue. She held out her arms as she walked. The snow was so gentle and soft and light, it almost made her forget about the house even as she walked toward it.

In her room, watched by the raven in the window – who was a stark contrast to the snowy skies and fields outside – she gathered the dried rose petals in a small bowl and crushed them with a pestle. She had found the tools in her explorations and hadn't had to borrow them from the kitchen. Her mother would not have approved.

She ran the bath as hot as it would go and filled a larger bowl, then stirred in the dried petals. The water instantly turned a very dark red, almost like blood. She watched it swirl in the bowl for a while, then set it at the windowsill. "You can't drink this," she told the raven. "It's not a tea."

The raven made a clicking sound. She wasn't sure if the bird approved. But it seemed necessary. The song still echoed in the deepest recesses of her head, and also the image of the uncle at the writing desk. The two things made her feel uncomfortable in entirely different ways.

As the bowl of water cooled, she ran a bath. The cold outside was getting stronger. Soon, she wouldn't be able to leave the window open, and she'd only see the raven when she could go out to the rose garden. She didn't like feeling sad about things like that. The raven regarded her like a guardian angel, and she wondered if it would hide away somewhere else when winter came full force.

She washed her hair with the red dye. It coated her white hair unevenly and much more brightly than the color of the water had suggested. Instead of blood red, she got a fiery pinkish color with hints of darker tones, but it was paler than she'd intended. Even the water in the tub took on the color she'd wanted. If she had been bathing in blood, though, it would've been thicker.

During her bath, the raven had flown off, and a bit of snow had gotten inside her room. She pulled the window closed. She'd have to let her hair dry on its own. She'd never get the color out of the towel. She wasn't sure she'd get the color off the skin of her shoulders and back, either.

She sat by the window watching the snow, careful not to get too close to her bed and spoil the sheets, waiting until her hair was dry enough to wrap up and stick a pin through before pulling on a white dress for supper. She didn't wear her hair up like that often, but her mother had given her hair pins for special occasions. They always felt excessively formal to Rosa, and she wasn't sure she ever wanted to be so formal, but if she ruined the dress her mother might kill her.

She examined herself in the mirror and decided she very much liked this new, redder version of herself. She pulled on her shoes and went downstairs to supper.

Her mother watched her walk into the dining room.

The uncles paused in their numerous conversations. For a moment, it seemed like every eye in the room turned to see her, to admire or admonish her. She felt unsafe under such scrutiny, but she stood straight, nodded once, and went to her chair without a word.

The uncles returned to their discussions of late harvests and early storms. Though they still didn't speak directly to her, they stole furtive glances in her direction. They made her nervous. She wasn't sure which had been the uncle at the writing desk. Some wore spectacles, some did not. The colors of their neckties were invariably grayish, but with different tints; several were that same reddish color, much less vibrant than her new hair color. Each time one looked at her, she could smell their attention, as if they radiated a strange kind of hunger.

Her mother looked at her but said nothing. She poured wine in both their glasses. She frowned, mostly, but once or twice the corners of her lips twitched in the other direction. A smile on her mother's face would look unclean and unreal. She couldn't quite manage it. Mostly, once they started eating, her mother didn't bother to look at her.

Supper was interrupted once. Outside, not too distant because otherwise they never would have heard it at all, a wolf howled. The sound echoed through the house and lasted a long time. Even the uncles went quiet. Her mother set her knife and fork down on the table. The howl stretched, and Rosa began to realize it was the same as one of the root chords of the watchmaker's piano song. He'd been playing a wolf's song and she hadn't noticed. No wonder it had made her so anxious.

When the howling stopped and a good three seconds had passed, Rosa's mother picked up her cutlery again and said, "The winter wolves will come closer to the house searching for food. Do not get yourself eaten, Rosa." Then she popped a piece of meat into her mouth, chewed, and followed it with a good swallow of red wine.

After supper, something happened that had never happened before. Rosa took her dishes to the sink and cleaned them, just as she did every night. But when she went to go upstairs to her rooms, two of the uncles had come out of the dining room and watched her progress from the hall. They seemed to have been in the midst of a conversation, but she was sure one of the words had been *red*. They quieted when she entered the hall, and didn't resume until after she'd climbed the stairs. She felt the weight of their eyes on her the whole time, and smelled the stench of their breath.

8.

That first winter was mild until late in the season. The land around them was often quiet, but once the snow started falling it never really stopped. Rosa didn't want to leave a path leading into the woods, so she watched from afar, often sitting in the rose garden or looking from her own window. The red faded from her hair in days, which disappointed her. The rose petal dye lingered longer in her skin and in the porcelain tub than in her hair. It faded before the days even got cold. The raven continued to visit.

Usually, she saw the bird in the garden, but she was beginning to understand its patterns. The raven lived in the woods somewhere, maybe near the gravestones because that made the most sense. Rosa didn't know what the raven ate. If she had a territory, it stretched to all horizons. She flew the perimeter of the house and its property. She swooped low when one of the uncles was visible in a window, and she responded to the sounds of wolves.

As her mother had warned, the wolves came closer to the house. Rosa found tracks near the vegetable garden. There seemed to be a number of them. It was possible the tracks belonged to something else, but what else lived in the forest and hunted in packs? Three or four times, usually at twilight, which came earlier every day, she thought she saw silhouettes against the edge of the forest. They were big and, if not white, gray enough to stand out against the dark wall of trees. One night, in the yard, seeing what might have been a wolf, let out a howl of her own. It cut the night. A huge flock of birds exploded from the forest trees, circled the house like a tornado, and returned to the woods.

It made her feel powerful.

Her mother came out onto the porch and gave her one of those looks. "What do you think you're doing? Get inside the house before you catch a chill."

Rosa had never caught a chill. Never in her whole life. Why would she now?

The cold inside and around the house was, in fact, sharper than any she'd experienced before. When the wind decided to kick up some action, it whistled through every gable and window frame and spire of the house.

At the supper table one night, her mother said, "It's the solstice. Have you prepared an offering?"

"Offering?"

Her mother frowned at her. The uncles went unnaturally quiet.

"We do want the days to get longer, do we not?"

"Well, yes."

"Then you'd better do something."

Her mother didn't explain what would make a suitable offering. Rosa went to her bedroom, found one of the hairpins, and returned with it to her mother. It was ornate with fancy red figures in fine brush strokes and writing in yet another language she couldn't comprehend. She put it on the table in front of her mother on a pile that had been gathered. The uncles had provided their own offerings: scraps of paper, dice, antique coins, a pair of spectacles without lenses, two dried roses of yellow and pink, and a piece of chocolate.

Rosa's mother removed her necklace, something she wore often, with a locket Rosa had never seen the inside of, and placed it ceremoniously on the pile. She bowed her head as if in prayer, mouthed words she didn't actually say, closed her eyes, and nodded once. "Okay, then, off to bed with you."

"I didn't do anything."

"With luck," her mother said, "this will be the longest night of the year. The moon will exhaust herself, and sunlight will return. Don't you want these things?"

"I guess."

"Then off to bed, and keep the lights out. I'll be shutting all the lights in the house so as to attract favors."

"Whose favors?"

Her mother shook her head, scowled, and pointed.

Reluctantly, Rosa returned to her rooms. Behind her, her mother was shutting all the lights, as though giving strength to the absolute darkness that held dominion inside these walls. Behind her mother, the uncles congregated, whispering amongst themselves and lingering in the fresh shadows.

Rosa locked the door to her rooms behind her.

She shut her lights, leaving not even a candle to read by, and sat in the big chair near the window. Far off in the forest, on the other side of that green and skeletal wall, she saw the reflections of bonfires so far away she'd never be able to reach them. She imagined people dancing around them, maybe singing, celebrating in a way other than locking themselves within a Stygian tenebrosity.

Despite the cold, she kept the window open. She listened to the sounds of the night, which were few. Too distant to hear the crackling fires, she was left to imagine those sounds. The wind made a little noise, but it wasn't severe tonight. With the nearly full moon, it was brighter outside than in her room. She played her fingers in the moonlight to throw shadow puppets across her bed, but the shapes were more abstract than she wanted.

Then a sound pierced the night. She heard it from the outside, but in fact she knew the piano was somewhere in the house. It was the same song, all those minor keys and that slow, meandering melody. It seemed appropriate. It played at her own emotions, but also personified the whole of the house, the properties around it, the gardens and the trees.

Once the song started, Rosa heard other sounds in the night as though someone had expanded the physical limits of her ears. She heard the whisperings of uncles inside, and the scratching of nails on wood. A large clock somewhere in the house ticked off the minutes. Her mother cried. *Cried.* Somewhere far and distant, her mother cried, and cried out – not noisily, not so that Rosa would usually hear it. In this house, her mother suffered. How had Rosa never noticed this?

She listened to her mother's rhythmic sobs, the slavering of hungry beasts, the murmurs drifting down from attics she had not yet discovered. She held her breath. She held her breath for a long time to better hear all the sounds of the house: the creaks in the wind, the footsteps that stopped outside her door, the uncles roaming the dark halls as though they had no need of light, and the clack of wolf claws on the wood floors.

Would the uncles let wolves into the house?

She went to her door and peered through the keyhole. It was impossible to see anything even under the best of circumstances. Now, she saw only darkness, obscurity, abysses – as though someone with an endlessly deep eye peered back at her. She stayed perfectly still. She wouldn't even blink, afraid she wouldn't be able to see the invisible eye anymore. She held her breath. She was getting good at that. She inhaled one time and held her breath for two counts of one hundred.

Finally, in a whisper, barely giving voice to the words at all, she asked, "Who's there?"

The darkness blinked. The other sounds stopped. Even her mother's crying ceased – or at least, Rosa could no longer hear it. She blinked, too, because her eye was dry, but she saw nothing more in the darkness. She felt no further presence.

At that same moment, she realized, the watchmaker's song had reached its final note. The echo of it only existed in her head now.

It was a long time before she was able to sleep. In the morning, she woke cold. She had left the window open. The raven had entered the room, more deeply than ever before. It had come onto her bed and perched on the blanket above her stomach where she slept. It carried something shiny in its black beak. It looked at her with its darker eye, dropped the gift, and flew out the window.

It was an old pocket watch on a chain. It was small, smudged with dirt and snow. Rosa didn't run water over the watch, but she did wipe it clean in the sink. Her towel came away with spots of crimson mud. The face of the watch was simple: a circle of Roman numerals, though not all of them were present. XII at the top, IIII, VII, and X. The others hadn't been rubbed away or lost to time; they had simply never existed. On the outside of the folding watch, a raven's profile had been engraved. It had been too encrusted in dirt to see that initially. The beak, the eye, the shape of the head – all mimicked her raven's exactly.

She rubbed it with her thumb. She wound the watch, but the mechanics inside refused to cooperate. Probably, there was too much dirt, or the gears had rusted. She didn't know how watches worked. But she knew someone who did.

She went looking for the room with the half door. That had been her only entry into the other house inside her house. The watchmaker had come out through a door to tend to the rose garden, but she hadn't ever seen that door again. She hadn't seen that room, either, but she made a renewed attempt.

She wandered halls, slipping past the uncles who seemed more and more frequently to be reading alone in hallways and sometimes lost in thought staring at old, fading landscape paintings. She recognized none of the artists and none of the lands in these. She imagined they were faraway fairy worlds, like the forest around the house, and that these paintings were somehow portals to these places if she could only unlock them.

Once or twice, she'd even searched the frames for keyholes.

This morning, though, she remained focused on her intention. She skipped the hall where the uncles seemed to live. She found several studies, a few sitting rooms, parlors, a conservatory, even an armory where racks on the walls had once upon a time carried rifles and pistols, maybe sabers, maybe epees. One silvery shield remained attached to the wall. She didn't try to remove it. It was bland and basic, without ornamentation, possibly the most simplistic thing in a house where even the silverware seemed intricately spun by hand.

Then she found the room. The furniture had been ignored and neglected. Everything looked delicate, especially the bureau, but she knew she could get behind it and open the half door into the other house.

It was a tighter squeeze than she remembered, but she got back there and tried to push the door open. It wouldn't budge. She tried the knob, but it wouldn't turn. Locked from the other side. She got onto her knees to peer through the keyhole.

The view wasn't spectacular. She saw little more than darkness on the other side, with just a hint of light spilling from a hallway. Down there, the watchmaker must be working, even now, and surely he would hear if she knocked.

Three times. She figured more would be rude, fewer would be insufficient. She gave three knocks, not gentle but not pounding, trying to find a balance between there. Then she waited.

She heard nothing from the other side of the door, but eventually a shadow slipped through the hallway light. The watchmaker stepped into the room and gave all his attention to the half door. He stood there, perfectly still, for far too long. She knocked again, three times again, as though it were a mystical number that would summon fairy kings and otherworldly princes.

Slowly, with deliberation, the watchmaker approached the door. Before he opened it, Rosa got back to her feet. She didn't want to be caught trying to spy. She heard him insert a key into the door. It turned in the lock, and after a moment clicked open. He withdrew the key. Turned the knob. Pulled the door in.

He bent over to look at her through the door, squinting as he did so, and said something in his foreign language. She'd forgotten that she couldn't understand a word of it. He asked a question, but he didn't move aside to let her in, and he seemed more annoyed than pleased to see her.

"Help," she said, holding out her hand. With the chain wrapped around two of her fingers, she let the pocket watch drop. It dangled in the air, spinning slowly. He looked at it. She frowned, and said, "Please."

He accepted the watch. He turned it over as he examined it, scrutinized it, gave it his full attention. He sighed gently, closed his fist around the watch, and nodded. He said something, though he must've known she didn't know what he was saying.

Then he slipped the watch into his pocket and closed the door.

The only thing she heard after that was the watchmaker locking the door. It sounded more intricate than any other lock in the house. After a moment, she knelt again and peered through the keyhole. At the hallway, he had stopped to withdraw the watch from his pocket and examine it again in the better light. He seemed to find it intriguing, at least. She hoped he would fix it and find a way to return it.

Over the next three days, she saw no sign of the watchmaker or the watch, but she didn't give up hope. She knew such work was intricate. She hadn't tried to open it herself because she didn't have the tools or the knowledge.

She kept mostly to her rooms, in fact. For a few hours every day, she went exploring, but the snow outside got thicker – and the uncles, inside, seemed also to get thicker.

Each, individually, remained tall and thin and pale, but there seemed to be more of them. At the supper table, in the parlor, in the study, even in the hall outside her room. She always locked her door, but she began taking special care to make sure not to accidentally forget. She remembered too distinctly the sounds of fingernails outside her door. She had merely imagined those hands trying the door, but it was not her imagination that the uncles looked at her more now.

She preferred when they never noticed her. Now, she felt like meat, an intrusion, and a nuisance, sometimes all at the same time. They still never talked directly to her. She would hear two of them speaking about her, though she rarely quite caught the words. They knew her name. They knew she had, for several days, pinkish hair that faded back into snow. When they walked, their feet made no sound, whether the floor was carpet or wood or tile. They made no eating sounds in the dining room, never seeming to touch the silverware, never clinking dishes, never smacking their lips or chomping their teeth.

She didn't know any of them individually. She couldn't pick out which had been at the writing desk. They were interchangeable, an entity as a whole, but it wasn't until after she'd given the pocket watch to the watchmaker – who was decidedly not one of the uncles, though that didn't tell her who he was – that one of them came into her room for the first time.

She had just pulled on a white dress in her closet, which was almost as big as the bathroom, though she didn't have nearly enough clothes to fill it, and came out into her bedroom. One of the uncles stood there, next to the bed, looking down at it no differently than if he'd been looking at a book in his hand. She thought she had locked the door. She stared at him a moment, still and silent, unmoving, unwavering, until he turned his head away from the bed to meet her eyes.

She screamed.

It wasn't a word. It was incoherent, but it was loud. She rarely screamed. She couldn't remember the last time; it must have been before coming to the house to live with the uncles and the rose garden. She screamed, and there was a response. Not in her room, not immediate, not in anything the uncle did. But her mother came running. *Running.*

Her mother never expressed emotion, but she looked almost frantic now. She threw her head about, taking in the scene, understanding everything. She ignored Rosa. Maybe that was a first, too. She went straight to the uncle, face to face, and kept her voice restrained. "You are violating our arrangement." When the uncle merely looked back at her, she added, "I would ask you to leave my daughter's room. *Now.*"

The uncle nodded once, then departed. He seemed almost to glide out of the room.

Her mother turned to Rosa, knelt in front of her and grabbed her by both shoulders. "Did he touch you?"

She shook her head.

"You will tell me if any of them do, won't you?"

"Yes, mother."

Her mother looked straight into her eyes, deeply, almost accusingly, searching for any sign of a lie. But Rosa wasn't lying, wasn't even trying to. She'd been startled, that was all. None of the uncles had ever been in her room before. He hadn't said anything or done anything but look around, and even that was limited.

Her mother, eventually, decided to believe her, which was a relief. Her mother didn't always believe. Rosa had learned to be quiet rather than risk saying something her mother would find unlikely.

"Good," she said, primping the shoulders and arms of Rosa's dress. "Are you ready for supper, then?"

"I am."

"Good." As they left the room, her mother made a show of locking the door. "I want you to keep your door locked at all times, do you understand me? Even when you aren't inside. I have a key. You can't lock me out. You don't have to worry about that."

After supper, in the dark of night and behind a locked door, Rosa heard three soft knocks at the door. She stiffened in her chair. She'd been watching the snow falling. Even gentle rapping on the door seemed a strong contrast to that. She took a breath before realizing the uncles wouldn't knock. Her mother wouldn't knock. There was only one real possibility. She went to the door, peered out the keyhole – but her door's keyhole never gave her much of a view of anything – then opened the door.

She looked down the hallway in both directions. There was no one and nothing. She looked at the floor, half expecting to find a silver tray, but found nothing. She frowned. That was disappointing. She hadn't expected anything in particular, but there shouldn't have been nothing.

She didn't see it until she went to shut the door: the pocket watch dangling and gleaming from the doorknob. She picked it up, snatching it off the doorway before one of the uncles came and tried to claim it. She gave another quick glance down the hall in both directions, then shut and locked her door.

She held the pocket watch to her ear and listened as it counted off the seconds.

CLOCKWORK RAVENS

9.

The watchmaker had cleaned and polished the pocket watch. It glistened like a jewel. The raven was more prominent and beautiful than she'd imagined. He'd removed every speck of dirt and dust from the face, and had probably done just as much and more with the mechanical guts. He'd even set the time properly.

She wrapped the chain around her hand and slept holding onto the watch. It was a gift, now, from the raven – who perhaps had etched her own face onto the casing – and the watchmaker, who had restored and revived it.

But in the morning, Rosa realized she needed to do something more to make it her watch and hers alone. Some of the uncles had pocket watches. That hers gleamed silvery instead of a dull gray was not enough to differentiate it. That it had absorbed the oils from her hands in the night wasn't enough.

In the bathroom, she climbed into the empty tub with the watch and her sewing needle. Quickly, carefully, she pricked her finger. It hardly hurt at all. A bead of blood instantly appeared. She pressed her thumb against the watch's raven face. She squeezed her thumb to draw another two drops and then smeared it against the silver.

With her thumb, she polished the watch's case, rubbing her blood into the pores of the metal, of the clockworks, until there was no sign of red anymore. It seemed to bring clarity to the etching. The raven's face had never looked so deep, so haunting, so real. Though the back was smooth, she rubbed her blood into that, too. When that wasn't enough blood, she pricked her palm three times. She marveled at the beauty of the pattern, the triangle – the pyramid she had created. Then she closed her fist over the chain and drew it through so that no part of the chain would be untouched. She did this several times, essentially giving the watch a part of her soul.

The watch seemed to appreciate it. Sure, it was an inanimate object; watches didn't have feelings or emotions or hungers or desires. But it seemed to not merely absorb but drink those spots of blood. The ticking was its heartbeat. It was a different rhythm than her own heart, but the watch wasn't human and shouldn't be expected to follow her lead. When she listened, the da-dum of her own heart and the tick-tock of the watch were, in fact, perfectly synchronized, timed so that the da- and the tick- always fell on the same beat.

Rosa smiled. She settled back, gripping the watch tightly, and for a while fell asleep in the porcelain bath. It gave her the strangest dreams, images of winter moons and wolves and trails of blood through the snow, but there was no plot, no thread to hold onto. After she woke, the images faded quickly. There'd been no warning and no story, only symbols she wasn't interested in interpreting. It was far better to enjoy the beauty than to seek the meaning.

When she went down for breakfast, a few of the uncles had congregated in the hall outside her room. Under their intense gazes, she locked her door and went downstairs. She kept the watch in a pocket of her dress and never planned to show it to anyone else. The uncles followed her to the dining room.

With the uncles so thick and unavoidable, she went outside to sit in the rose garden. The uncles rarely seemed to leave the house. She didn't know how their dealt with the commodities and textiles. She sat on one of the stone benches and wished more of the roses were in bloom. There was too much snow, too many icicles dripping from the demi-statues of goddesses and queens, and just too much cold for all but the strongest, most vibrant roses to peek at the world.

The only bush that seemed to have more than one or two blooms, and maybe the only roses that were fully opened and glistening in the sunlight, were white. She thought they were pure white, but realized the petals were actually lined, very thinly, with black on the outside. Like eye makeup.

Her mother would never allow her to play with makeup, but that's how she would have done it. A little bit of black, a little bit of red.

One rose, only one in the entire garden, was black all the way through. Every petal, every fold, even the smell of it seemed darker, richer, more fragrant.

She knew what the watchmaker would do. She retrieved shears, then said to the black rose: "I think you're beautiful, just the way you are, but I suspect you'll infect the garden and steal all the other colors."

The bloom trembled. It was as open and full and bright as could be, coated with icy dew so that it almost seemed a skin. She didn't want to hurt the flower, but she saw no other choice. She followed the stem to its lowest point and snipped.

A thorn bit her as she did so.

"That's fair," she said. The thorn cut her palm, near the pyramid she had etched herself. It was a scratch, rather than a poke, and bled more thickly and wetly. She held her hand over the rose and squeezed her fist until a few drops fell on the black petals. They mixed with the dewy icicles, melting them, and caused the petals to wilt. The petals absorbed the blood, like the pocket watch had. Only one drop fell into the snow at her feet.

The pain of the thorn was greater than that of the needle, but it was somehow a pleasant pain, comfortable, welcoming. There had been no other way for her to bond with the rose even as she executed it. That pain, not the physical, brought a tear to her eye. Just the one. It was enough.

When she looked up, she saw the raven watching from the top of one of the statues, and she saw uncles in one of the windows of the house, and she saw wolves silhouetted against the forest.

She focused, instead, on the dying rose. "I don't want to crush you," she said. She brought the flower into the house through the front doors. She passed uncles who seemed to notice her by scent. They sniffed at the air, curled their noses in response to an odor – maybe the perfume of the rose. She carried it to her room, locked the door behind her, and put the rose in her wood box. She put the pocket watch there, too. She didn't think it was safe to carry with her all the time. She didn't want to lose or break it.

It was the first of the raven's gifts she hadn't sewn into a secret place in her dress.

10.

The winter was mild until the very end of it, when a storm pummeled the house and buried the rose garden. Over three horrifying nights, the wind whipped against Rosa's windows, caused the house to shudder from foundation to attic, and agitated her uncles. They chittered more, speaking faster but less coherently. Her mother made a fire in the parlor's big fireplace. The bricks of the hearth were the same as those outside of the house, as though section of it had turned inside out. The chimney sucked smoke out of the house.

The raven found shelter inside the house. Rosa saw her in the hallway when she went to bed the first night. The next day, however, the uncles found the raven and tried to chased her out. It was absurd, watching her uncles race around the house trying to catch and kill the bird. She had never seen them so animated. One might be standing in the hall examining some regal portrait when suddenly he caught sight of the raven in his peripheral vision and launched after it. They made strange sounds as they did this, something between the raven's caw and a high-pitched scream. They chased the raven with their books, with umbrellas, with their hands. Rosa had no doubt they would simply snap her neck if they caught her.

But the raven was swift, and she seemed to know her way around the house. She ducked into rooms and disappeared for hours at a time. Unless the uncles actually saw her, they seemed to ignore the raven.

Her mother, however, complained about it. "They'll take

care of that *bird.*" She said it like a curse, like it was vermin of some sort, spreading dangerous diseases and death with its filthy beak and claws. She didn't race after the bird. One time, when the bird flew into the parlor, she wielded the fireplace poker like a weapon, but never thrust or swung it. She seemed to be challenging the bird to come close enough so that she didn't have to do any work.

Rosa and her mother spent a lot of time in the parlor those few days. The fire was the best source of heat for the whole house. The uncles wandered in and out at random. There were multiple doors, so there was always another way for her to go, should Rosa wish to escape.

When the winter storm finally calmed, when the house settled and the uncles seemed to relax, Rosa spent most of the day in her rooms. Outside, the landscape had been utterly changed by mounds of snow. The snow was as deep as she was tall. She confirmed this when she ventured onto the porch. She didn't want to get lost in the snow. It wasn't like the forest. She'd never find her way back. The rose garden had been obliterated. Only a few of the higher statues stuck their heads out of the snow drifts.

From her rooms, she watched the blanched sky, the streaks of white and gray clouds gliding swiftly past, the shuddering of the forest. At one point, the raven returned to Rosa's room, landed at her closed window, and tapped her beak on the glass.

She let the bird out. She was the darkest, blackest, most vibrant spot of color against the remnants of the blizzard. She disappeared in the direction of the forest. Rosa wondered how the wolves had managed during the storm and where they might have hidden.

When Rosa went to shut the window, she noticed something outside, a slash of black in the snow below her room. She shut the window and hurried outside to retrieve it before the wind or the snow or one of the uncles snuck out there first. It was one of the raven's feathers. Had it been an intentional gift, or just something that dropped naturally?

She had to detour around one of the uncles in the hallway to get outside. Usually, they wouldn't seem to notice her, but in this case he gave a whimsical little laugh. When she looked back at him, his eyes on her were unrelenting. She slowed down, staring at those gray eyes with the fleck of amber in them, the same color she could find in her own eyes but in much more abundance. He smiled, slowly, but it wasn't a joyful smile. He said, "Good day, *Rosa*." He enunciated the syllables of her name, rolled the R, seemed to taste her in the sound of her name. She took a breath, nearly tripped, and ran the rest of the way.

The feather lay undisturbed on top of the snow, where it hadn't even made an impression. She picked it up and, in the cold, examined it. It was better than trying to get past the uncle again.

Rosa always believed the raven was thoroughly black, although she sometimes thought she saw other colors in her feathers. Now, she was sure. The feather was mostly black, especially at the end, shot through with some deep blues and indigoes that reminded Rosa of the night sky immediately after dusk. She could almost see stars in the feather.

The wind was still fierce, and the sky gray to the point of threatening, so Rosa went back inside but through a different door. She still saw uncles. They seemed to be everywhere. Most went about their business and ignored her. Only two or three turned to look at her. Only the one, earlier, had given her that faux smile.

She added the feather to her wood box. She took a moment

to caress a petal of the rose, then opened the watch to check the time. The numbers seemed odd, but she remembered they'd always been odd. Had her blood seeped into the innards of the watch? She wound the watch with some degree of care, feeling for the tension that indicated it had been fully wound. Its rhythm still matched hers. She hoped that would never change.

Weeks and months passed before she saw the raven again. She began to fear it had died. The winter snows melted, spring erupted, and the fields went wild with flowers she had never seen, painting the world around her like some chromatically chaotic landscape. The roses all came back to life, flourishing in the spring, with brilliant reds, whites, oranges, and pinks. Insects buzzed around the house, animals other than wolves were visible in the fields, and of course Rosa wanted to get back into the woods.

First was her mother's birthday. Breakfast was an enormous feast, as always, and the uncles attended in great numbers. Three or four of them took turns dancing with her mother in the parlor, in front of the hearth gone dark. While others watched the dance, a few watched Rosa instead. One extended a hand, asking to dance without actually asking. Rosa shook her head. She was enjoying the music, a waltz, playing on the record player. It sounded so distant but so wondrous, like another world where fairies pranced in the sunshine and ran from terrible twilight beasts. She would've asked her mother the name of the song, but she seemed to be having too good a time. She'd been drinking more wine than usual. It was her first birthday in the house. They'd been there almost a year. Rosa thought she even saw her mother kiss one of the uncles on the cheek.

It was as good a time as any to run for the forest.

One of the uncles stood at the back door. He hadn't been

waiting for her, was as surprised to see her as she was to see him. He smiled. They could still hear the music, so he held out a hand. "Dance," he said. It was an imperative. He wasn't asking, he wasn't suggesting, and he wasn't kind about it. He held out his hand and expected her to take it.

"I can't dance," she said.

"A young lady should dance," he said, still holding the hand out.

She shook her head, backed a step away. "I'd rather not."

"I didn't ask."

He took a step forward.

Rosa didn't know what to do. If she ran back, she would spoil her mother's mood, and that would mean trouble for her. If she refused, he seemed likely to chase her, to force her, to punish her for it. She couldn't imagine what form of punishment he might deliver. None of the uncles had ever done such a thing.

So she put her hand in his.

He squeezed, not gently, and pulled her closer. Then together, in the hall, to the distant waltz, they danced – one two three – his hand on hers and the other at the small of her back. The dance was interminable. The music played for all of ever, and ever after that as well, even if it was just a couple of minutes. When it finally ended, the song and the dance, she withdrew from the uncle, curtsied with feigned civility, and said, "Thank you, uncle."

He smiled.

She raced around him, through the door, out onto the porch and away from the house. The forest waited. It seemed to breathe for her as she got closer. She didn't usually run to it; she'd never run in quite this way before. She found her entry point through the thick, lush greenery and went into the woods.

It was like another world. Every time, the woods revealed a

different aspect of themselves to her. She saw life everywhere, from leaves unfurling to insects like little twigs to beetles and spiders and worms in the earth. Every color seemed rich and wet and nearly glistening.

She wandered with her mouth open, awe on her tongue and on her fingertips. She didn't seem to have a direction, but she reached the small graveyard, those dozen stones – no, only eleven. One had disappeared.

It wasn't one of the bigger ones. But the row that had been five was now only four, and there was a space where there should have been a stone. It wasn't that it had fallen over; it had been taken away entirely. There was no sign of it, no tracks through the dirt, no sign it had been carried or dragged.

"Why?" she asked.

No one and nothing answered. None of the other stones seemed to be any different than before. They still bore the same unpronounceable names. While Rosa sat amongst the stones, the raven returned. She landed on the biggest of the stones. She carried something in her talons. She cawed, dropped it, and waited.

It was a length of red ribbon.

"Thank you," she said, picking it up and tying it in her ghost-white hair. She couldn't wear it back into the house. Her mother, even deep into her wine on her birthday, might notice and disapprove.

"I want to dye my hair red again," she told the raven. "Do you know what I did wrong last time? Why it only lasted a few days?"

The raven didn't know. Her mother might, but she'd never tell. And Rosa wasn't going to shatter her mother's mood by trying tonight. She needed to gather more roses petals, anyhow, darker in color if she could manage. No pink this time. Red, and if possible, black.

On her way back home, she picked hawthorn berries, and carried them by lifting the front of her dress to make a scoop. They were red, very red, like blood, and like the color she wanted in her hair. Maybe if she added some of these to the mixture, she'd get the color she wanted.

CLOCKWORK RAVENS

11.

A month later, Rosa tried to color her hair again. She did it basically the same way as before, except this time she boiled water in the kitchen, and she also crushed the dried berries into her rose petals. Only red and darker this time. She'd found some violet, bluer but still tinged with red, but no black roses over those few weeks.

The uncles roamed the halls. She managed to avoid her mother, so she didn't have to explain what she was doing, even though she didn't think her mother would stop her. By now, spring was in full effect, with its pollens and whirlwind of flowers, the bees and hummingbirds, rabbits racing through the fields, mice avoiding the hawks. The raven seemed unperturbed, so Rosa hadn't let any of it bother her. She brought the water up to her room in a teapot and poured some into a bowl with the dry ingredients she'd thoroughly crushed with her pestle. She let the water cool, but not all the way this time, and she didn't bother filling the tub. She didn't want to risk diluting the mixture. She added only enough water to make it a paste. The color was beautifully dark and resonant, closer to what she wanted than last time. It smelled of roses and the forest. She filled her hands with the goop and ran them through her hair. She spent an hour on it, making sure to be thorough, to get every strand from top to bottom. She might have liked the way her hair looked almost white, but it reminded her too much of the uncles.

She washed her hands and her shoulders, holding her hair

up with the one remaining hairpin. It was a deep, blood red on her skin. She couldn't remove every trace of it. It had gotten under her skin, had perhaps connected to her veins underneath. The streaks in her hair weren't perfect. They weren't entirely uneven, but the colors shifted more than she'd hoped. It was darker than it had been last time, but still not the rich merlot color she wanted. It felt like her hair refused it.

The raven sat at her window. Next time, maybe, she should use raven feathers – though Rosa only had one, maybe the bird would give her a couple if she asked. She'd never actually asked for anything before. The raven's gifts were always a surprise. Black hair, even infused with glistening indigoes, wouldn't be so vibrant as blood, but would definitely be an improvement over ghost.

She let her hair drop, shook it out, looked at herself in the mirror, and smiled. It wasn't quite right, but it was lovely anyhow. Gleaming and luscious and otherworldly. She felt like she could go into the woods and commune with the wolves in the forest, with the voles in the fields, with the fairies in their secret lands.

At the table during supper, her mother looked but said nothing about the hair. The uncles looked and said nothing, but then they looked some more. Maybe Rosa was doing something wrong.

Over the next few weeks, months, and even years, her life became a series of little wanderings between dying her hair darker and darker shades of red. The color rarely lasted more than a week before fading to pink. She explored the forest but never found a portal to Avalon. She ran through the fields, the flowers and the corn, and stayed outside as much as possible during the warmer months. Her mother complained about the mud on her dresses, but Rosa cleaned them, and sewed them when necessary. During the winters, the snow piled higher every year, the wolves sounded closer, and more than a few times the wind managed to break into the house through unattended windows. The raven sometimes sheltered in her rooms, though Rosa never actually saw a nest. The raven continued to bring little gifts: a marble, an old jack, a rusted nail, the nib of a fountain pen.

She had to evade the uncles more. They came more and more to the hall outside her room, often three or four of them at a time, and there seemed never to be a time when at least one wasn't out there. They watched her always now. So did her mother. Rosa went to the forest less but still explored the house. Slipping away from the uncles was easy because they never, except that one winter day with the raven inside, moved with any real speed or apparent deliberation. She couldn't imagine the things they thought. Their conversations, amongst each other, still consisted primarily of politics, textiles, opera, and baseball. She cared for none of these, except perhaps opera, but she had never actually heard one. She asked her mother about it once.

"Oh, no," her mother said. "Such things are not for us."

"Why not?"

"They're *obscenities*," her mother said. "Like all music, and also dancing, operas should be confined to prostitutes and courtesans, and the vague, loathsome men who enjoy their company."

"The uncles talk about operas."

Her mother smiled then. It was a mean smile. "That merely proves my point, doesn't it?"

She didn't point out that her mother danced at least twice every year, listening to music, as they celebrated birthdays.

The night before her seventeenth birthday, in the forest, no longer afraid to get caught and very nearly defiant, Rosa found herself face to face with one of the winter wolves. It was early for the wolf, technically, being a young autumn. Its whitish gray fur would've camouflaged it perfectly in the snow. As it was, the wolf had snuck up on her without a sound and without being seen.

Its head came almost as high as her chest, but its body was immense and lean and muscular. It didn't remind Rosa of the fairy tales at all. When she saw it, she'd been leaning over a patch of wildflowers. She rose to her full height, which was not imposing. She had always been small and thin and seemingly frail, but she knew she was strong and fast – just not wolf strong or wolf fast. Her hair was a very light shade of pink, and her dress far too clean considering she'd been frolicking in the forest. Only the hem, really, was dirty at all.

The wolf regarded her. The wolf's breath was rhythmic, like her heart and like the watch in her pocket. The wolf huffed and stepped one front paw closer to her.

Rosa held her breath. "I don't know how to speak with you," she admitted. The wolf seemed not to care. "But I wish we could be friends." The wolf seemed to wish no such thing. The wolf moved another step closer.

Rosa held her ground. She avoided confrontations with her mother and the uncles whenever she could, but she'd grown incapable of fear. Only the watchmaker made her afraid, and only because he lived in parts of the house she could almost never access. Even still, she was starting to feel something akin to fear at the base of her bones. She would run, but she wouldn't get far. She'd rather face the wolf if it indeed to consume her.

She took a breath. "I'd rather you didn't eat me, Sir Wolf."

The wolf sniffed again, coming closer, touching her shoulder and stomach with its nose and drawing in deep inhalations.

When the wolf looked into her eyes, she saw its teeth, rows of them under the black skin of its snout, and she saw eyes not unlike hers, with a touch of amber. When the wolf looked into her eyes, and reflected the color of her own, she smiled. She said, "We are related, you and I."

The wolf blinked softly, then sat, then yawned.

Slowly, quietly, Rosa walked away from the seated wolf. It watched, and she gave it more of her attention than the path in front of her. She still, all these years later, exited the forest through the same break in the brush indicated by her fraying, faded piece of string.

The wolf made no move to follow her. She knew wolves were rarely loners, and suspected an entire pack of them laid in wait just beyond her peripheral vision, but none struck out at her, and none followed her from the cover of the trees.

She walked slowly, calmly, even patiently across the field halfway to the house. She listened to the precarious soundless forest. She glanced over her shoulder. That's when she realized the wolves had, in fact, followed her from the forest, and there were at least a dozen of them. Only half were nearly as big as the wolf she had met; the others made up for their size by their numbers, by their strength, by the power of their teeth.

Rose broke into a run. She had meant to collect berries. She had meant to visit the graveyard. She had meant to commune with the trees. Instead, she ran for her life. But the house was forever away, an eternity across grassy fields abuzz with dragonflies that could not defend her from predators of any size.

She ran, pumping all her strength through her legs, panting, straining, unreservedly. She didn't look back until she had cut the distance to the house by another quarter.

The wolves were right behind her.

One of the uncles was directly ahead of her. She almost

didn't see him. She almost ran straight into them. Both would've tumbled to the ground and become nothing but wolf's food. She stopped at the last moment. He brushed her aside. He was as gray and gaunt and dusty as any of the uncles, but he was outside – they were never outside – and he stood facing the wolves as though he knew it was a fight he would win.

The wolves seemed to know it too. They stopped their chase. They paced side to side at a respectable distance. When they had done this for half of forever, the uncle grabbed Rosa by the wrist – he didn't take her hand, but gripped her with an impossible unbreakable strength – and dragged her the rest of the way to the house. He moved fast. She couldn't get her feet under her. At the steps to the porch, he pulled her up and practically yanked her arms from its socket. He held her before him, looked at her with fiery eyes, and said, far more calmly than she would have expected, "Wolves are bad."

"I know."

He still held her. Her hand had gone white. Her bones hurt from the pressure. He nearly had her suspended over her own feet. He looked back, once, to be sure the wolves hadn't gotten brave, then returned all his attention to her. "The wolves would have killed you."

"I know." She was near tears, but wouldn't give in. The pain of his grip was unbearable.

He said one last thing: "*You owe me your life.*" Then he let her go.

She scrambled all the way to her rooms. She shut and locked the door, washed her face, saw that her dress had been ruined beyond repair – and that she had lost the pocket watch. Her raven's finest gift. It must've fallen from her pocket while the uncle dragged her. She fell to her knees then and buried her face in the torn dress still in her hands.

The raven knocked at the window frame. Rosa often left it open so the bird would be free to come and go as she wished. The raven knocked, saw she'd been noticed, and flew away, leaving another gift. It wasn't the pocket watch retrieved from her flight, though she'd hoped it might be. It was a knife.

The blade was open, but folded back into the handle. It was sharp. She ran her finger along the edge and drew a thin line of blood from her skin to test it. The blade was short, thick, and straight, the handle black and possibly bone. She weighed it, then slashed it slowly a few times in front of her. It was heavy enough to feel powerful in her hand. This wasn't something she could sew into one of her dresses.

She'd had to move the button and the earring and other gifts into different dresses as she got older and bigger.

She put the knife in her box, but she thought about it all night, and was still thinking about it the next morning when she went down for her birthday breakfast.

Her mother smiled as she presented the feast. All the uncles seemed to be in attendance. She could hardly concentrate on what her mother was saying. Something about years, agelessness, timelessness, and generations. She spoke about her own mother, whom Rosa had never met. "Autumn birthdays are special," she said, but if she ever explained why, Rosa didn't catch it.

Rosa sat for a while in the rose garden. She read a book of poetry from the library. She might have read it before. The library had hundreds of books, but not more than that. It hardly seemed sufficient for a lifetime. Some were written in other languages, and yes, some were written with the language of the gravestones. She tried to work her way through these but couldn't. Even when there were illustrations, often elaborate and finely detailed, she couldn't discern the relationship between those and the words. There were patterns and repetitions. She thought she might be smarter later. She kept one of those books, a thinner one, in her rooms, and every few weeks she opened it and worked her way through the words without ever understanding one of them.

The days had started growing cooler earlier this year. She couldn't sit in the garden into the night. Some nights over the summer, she'd image sleeping on that stone bench. When the statues came to life and started dancing, as they must've done every night because no one wants to be trapped in a single pose forever, she might dance with them, and thus learn the secrets of that strange language. She might learn about herself, too, and about the fairies she'd never seen in the forest, and the woodsmen who sometimes chopped trees so distantly she only ever heard the echoes of their axes.

She watched the forest. It seemed further away now, as though it had retreated to the edges of the horizon. She didn't see the wolves, but could smell the stench of the big one's breath. It had seemed almost nonthreatening for a moment. If she'd had the knife yesterday, she wouldn't have been afraid. She could have stood her ground against the wolf, showed him her blade, and forced him back into the shadows.

The watchmaker came out of the house through his secret disappearing door. He walked a little more slowly, but he wasn't as old – nor as thin, as gray, as gaunt, as ghastly – as the uncles. She rarely saw him. He came to the rose garden. Her heart skipped a beat. She liked to talk to him, or to listen – because he spoke the language of the gravestones.

"Hello!" she said when he'd gotten close enough.

He looked at her and smiled. Was it possible that no one else in the house knew he lived there? His own rooms and hallways seemed to have been folded inside the rooms and hallways she and her mother shared. She'd never seen the watchmaker and the uncles in the same room. She wondered if his house was somehow the inside-out version of her own, everything inverted and reversed and hidden. She wondered why she'd been able to find it, as infrequently as she had. "Good morning," she said when he was closer.

He had an old leather notebook in his hands. He sat beside her, untied the twine holding the book shut, and opened it to reveal a mess of papers, some bound but some loose, and a small collection of colored pencils. On the first pages, he – or someone – had sketched the insides of watches and clocks, cogs and sprockets, wheels, pinions, gears, and screws. There were astronomical charts, and plenty of notes on the sides with letters that matched those on the graves.

There were maps, too, of places she had never seen or known, and an intricate, precise drawing of the front of the house, with all its windows and architectural flourishes, the statuary she sometimes forgot about, the porch and the doors. Some of the lines ran beyond the boundaries of the house, straight lines with little blue numbers sketched beside them.

When he went to turn the page, she stopped him. He asked something, but seemed to answer it himself, and waited.

She counted the windows. The gables. The dormers. She stared hard at the picture, because it was definitely her house – but it wasn't, not at all. It was his, his house within hers, and it was different.

"There's not enough windows," she said, pointing at three together on one side. "The house isn't long enough."

He smiled. He couldn't understand her any more than she understood him.

She removed her hand and nodded. "Go on," she said.

On further pages, there were more clockwork designs. Some

resembled spiders. Spindles. Compasses and roses. Then, there was the raven face from her pocket watch, and on the same page the guts of her watch.

She paused a moment and looked out into the field. Could she find it? Had she dropped it near the house or far from it? Had the grass eaten it? Mice run off with it? Rabbits stole away with it into their holes? Had the wolves taken the watch as a symbol of the prey they had lost?

The watchmaker looked out into the field, following her gaze, and shook his head sadly as he said something maybe meant to be comforting. He was a fountain of advice and knowledge and wisdom, if only she could discern it. He seemed to be saying that things lost were gone, and would only be returned in their own time. It made so much sense. Impulsively, she hugged him.

This wasn't something she did. Or something he did. He lifted his hands so as not to touch her and looked startled. She didn't hold him long. When she retreated, he smiled again, then returned his attention to the book. He pointed at something inside the sketched mechanisms of her watch. It seemed like even the insides had been arranged to resemble the raven etched on the case.

Further into the sketchbook, the plans and sketches became more complicated, and it was no longer just watches and clocks but ballerinas in boxes, a miniature upright piano with a mouse seated at it, a monkey with a violin, a carousel with four horses, a ladybug, and finally a raven.

"What's that?" she asked, pointing, to stop him from turning the pages. There was brief sketch of the raven's profile similar to that on her watch. There were the makings of a mechanical eye. An intricately designed feather.

He shook his head and said something wistful. The tone

suggested this wasn't something he'd made yet, only a sketch, a plan, a hope and a dream. Maybe an intention. At the bottom of the page was a single word in his unknowable language. "Is that the word for raven?" she asked. But it was too many characters. She couldn't decipher the language merely by assigning her lettering to those symbols; their words, and the spelling of those words, would also differ. She'd been going about it all wrong, and now she doubted she'd ever be able to figure it out. There were too many complications. If the word for watch was *clock* and the word for clock *uhr*, she would be forever lost without a guide. As many things as the watchmaker might have been, he had never been a translator.

He said something, a sentence, an explanation of sorts, as he closed and re-tied the book. He carried it with reverence. He said something that might have meant *happy birthday*, but might just as easily have meant *goodnight* or *till we meet again* or *don't play with the wolves, they'll eat you and forget you before they're finished digesting*. He rose, and returned to the house, entering through his secret door.

She watched him, then thought about following him.

He hadn't indicated that she should, but the existence of the door might be an invitation. It wasn't just a regular door, it was plain and not very imposing. Four wood panels, a simple knob. It wasn't locked. It turned easily for her. She pulled it open and entered a basement.

She had never found a basement in the house, though she had known one existed.

It wasn't like the other doors into the house, which were all raised a few steps above the ground. This one descended, leading to someplace pungent and fertile. The floor was black soil, but at first it seemed like nothing grew here. That was wrong. There were clumps of toadstools, orange capped mushrooms, and yellow lichen on the walls. The basement wasn't overrun with these things. It wasn't a garden of luminescent delights. Each spot of fungus and flora was unique, but they were tiny and sparse. She had to be careful to not accidentally trample through fragile regal caps or twined tentacles bursting from the soil.

The basement seemed as wide and as deep as the entire house. Darkness swallowed its furthest reaches. In places, a spear of fungi shaped like a vase glowed lightly blue, or a venous conflagration of a faint red. None of them actually emitted any light, but they provided her a means of navigating the basement.

Some of the mushrooms were gray, and though only a few inches high, shared the lean, gaunt features of the uncles. She realized, then, this wasn't the basement the watchmaker had walked into. Doors in this house were tricky; they might not always lead to the same places.

That gray patch of mushrooms were grayer than her uncles, and lacked faces, but if she squinted and imagined them taller, carrying books or wearing spectacles, dapper and sophisticated in their three piece suits, with ties and pocket squares, buttons and belts, collars and cuffs – they were so much like her uncles, she startled herself and fell over backwards. She landed next to another patch of fungi, these arranged like a wild forest in miniature.

She crawled away from those, careful not to get too close, afraid the fungal forest might be expanding. She felt the weight of its breath behind her, on her legs, the small of her back, the nape of her neck.

She reached the door and scrambled outside again. The sun was pale, the sky chalky, but the air carried the fragrance of roses and the distant howling of wolves. That distance made her feel safe. The door behind her – it wasn't really there, wasn't a door at all, merely a wall of the house below windows.

Rosa retrieved her book from the garden, thanked the statues for the dances they would later share, and intended to retreat all the way to her rooms.

Three uncles waited at the front door when she walked in. They loomed around her, seemed to swell with her presence. Unambiguously, their eyes focused the weight of all their attention on her. One shook his head. One grinned. It wasn't fair to call it a smile anymore; the uncles had never smiled.

Their presence turned her away from the big staircase. She raced toward the dining room, toward the parlor, toward another stairway, but the hallways were lined with uncles, and all of them seemed to be fully intent on her.

One reached out.

She spun away, circled into the parlor, where her mother sat in a chair near the cold hearth. She looked up, and she also grinned. "It's your birthday," she said. "I have chosen a record."

It was already on the record player waiting for the needle to find the groove.

Uncles poured into the parlor from all sides. They sniffed at the air. They seemed to crowd the room. Rosa's mother frowned. She said, "Be a dear and chase away the silence, won't you, Rosa? It is your birthday, after all."

Rosa stood there breathing, each inhalation deeper than the last. Her hands had curled themselves into fists. She didn't know when that had happened.

"Why do we live in this house?" she asked.

"It's our house," her mother said.

"Why?"

"It was my mother's house, and her father's before her, and it goes back a hundred generations or more. We have always lived in this house."

"But we haven't," Rosa said. "We used to live somewhere else."

"Where was that?"

"In a village, right?" Rosa asked. She wasn't sure. She remembered arriving, but she didn't really remember much before that.

"Stop with these silly notions," her mother said, "and either turn on the music, or lock yourself in your room without supper, without dessert. And I prepared a special dessert for your birthday, Rosa, dear."

Rosa pushed through the uncles to get at the record player. She lowered the needle. She listened to the static-filled rhythm of the record underneath the music. It seemed more resonant than all the instruments combined: the scratch, scratch, scratch of the needle on vinyl, as though the scratch and hiss was a song of its own, something underneath the melody trying to break through, trying to be heard.

She was sure they had lived somewhere else before, but she remembered nothing about it, nothing about the place and the people who must've been there, nothing about her father except that he'd died, nothing about her past except that she was sure she had one.

Later, after supper, after a dessert of delicious macerated strawberries, Rosa locked herself in her rooms, sat at the window watching the pale, bleached sky, and thought it odd that the uncles had no names.

She heard them outside her room, pacing like wolves, hungry and predatory. Their footfalls echoed more than silence, like absence, as though the soundlessness of the uncles drowned all the sounds of the world. She opened her window and she opened her box; the crystal black rose, frozen and dried and bled so many years ago; the raven's feather; the knife; the empty place once occupied by her watch. She let one tear fall for the watch, then picked up and opened the knife.

The blade was sharp. She drew it lightly across her forearm. A red line formed. It hurt, but it was a beautiful kind of hurt, and she didn't dig the blade deeply enough to hit any major arteries. When she squeezed her fist, the line welled up, droplets formed, two big and one small, and one of these rolled down the side of her arm. The red was so brilliant, so vibrant, so pretty – it mesmerized her. It was the red she'd always wanted in her hair but never seemed to be able to get. It was like hawthorn berries or the plushest of the roses. The pain underneath gave it substance and depth. She tightened her fist again, drew another line across the first, and watched the blood bubbling up. That might be the wolves next time, should they try again to chase her down. She frowned. That hadn't been fair. She'd only ever been good to the forest, quiet and respectful. The big wolf had seemed to accept her, yet they chased her anyway and would've devoured her if one of the uncles hadn't been there to rescue her.

That made it less than fair. One of the uncles – she didn't even know which – had something over her, something that never should have been there to have. With one last squeeze, she drew a half dozen beads of blood from her slices, and this made her smile.

CLOCKWORK RAVENS

12.

For a while, the house was quiet. Rosa walked through the fields searching for her watch, keeping an eye out for the raven, watching for wolves in one direction and uncles in the other. She spent time in the rose garden. The statutes never seemed to move or change, but she knew one day if she was careful she'd catch one slipping in her peripheral vision. She never saw the watchmaker, though one night she heard his song on the piano.

It was strange, that he never played anything else. Maybe he actually played every night, and no other song could reach her.

One night, wandering the halls of the house, evading the uncles and her mother, she entered a sitting room of some sort. This might've been the exact opposite side of the house to her own rooms. The windows looked out onto the rose garden.

And there, in the light of the full moon, was her mother.

It was strange, seeing her mother sitting in her private space, on the stone bench she often read at, surrounded by the demi-statues of goddesses and goat men who were meant to conduct Rosa to a fairy dance hall.

But maybe it wasn't her mother? The woman wore a white dress far more similar to the style Rosa wore than her mother. She sat facing away from the house, so Rosa could only see the woman's back. She had her mother's slimness, but so did Rosa. The woman might have been anyone, and she might only be visible in the light of the moon.

The full moon was strong that night, stronger perhaps than any other. Rosa watched the woman and wondered, briefly, if she'd still be there if Rosa ran downstairs to the garden. She might also have been a ghost, a reflection of who her mother had been or even who Rosa might become, or maybe neither of them. Maybe she belonged to the house inside her house, and lived with the watchmaker.

As long as Rosa watched, the woman simply sat in the moonlight. But clouds drifted across the sky. When they obscured the moon even briefly, when the light failed to reach the rose garden, it was like the woman wasn't even there.

During one of those patches of darkness, Rosa realized one of the uncles stood beside her also looking out the window. He seemed sad. The uncles never seemed sad. They never really expressed any emotions. When she looked at him, he turned to look at her, nodded briefly, then returned to the window. The clouds had cleared, at least momentarily, and the moon's light flooded the rose garden, but there was no sign of the woman.

Her mother was, in fact, downstairs, in the parlor, reading a book and wearing her normal style of dress, and looked as though she'd never seen a stray strand of moonlight in her life.

The next full moon, Rosa sat on the porch and watched the rose garden. A slight wind caused her to shiver. There'd been no rain for weeks, but the air now carried ice crystals so small, Rosa only saw them when she tilted her head and squinted in just the right way.

Where she sat, she couldn't be seen from any of the windows. As far as anyone inside the house was concerned, she might be a thousand miles away, perhaps on a beach or in the mountains, or deep under the earth where only gnomes and miners lived. She had her knife in a pocket, just in case. Nights had been growing cold and unsteady. There might be visitors. There had never been a visitor, but there was always the chance. There might be wolves, though they'd never come this close to the house. And there might be uncles, whom she knew were not, in fact, bound within those walls.

The raven perched on the porch rail near her and kept watch over the rose garden. She hardly moved. It was too early in the season for her to disappear, but she would, soon enough and perhaps too soon. The raven gave her a sense of well-being, as though the psychopomp protected her from forces unseen. The dark hid the bird entirely, but Rosa would never forget its nearness. She felt the quick rhythm of its heart.

Rosa waited for the woman to reappear. She wanted to see her more closely. How many times had she missed the visitation simply because she'd been at a window on the wrong side of the house? Her mother was in the parlor, most likely, and the uncles wandered thickly through the halls. Once upon a time, they had remained mostly in their rooms, coming out for meals but only five or six at a time. She was sure, now, there were a hundred of them, but she'd been unable to count. They were too similar to each other. The subtle change in the shape of spectacles, or a minor skin blemish near the corner of one's eye, was difficult to track. She had started counting at the dining table one night when a dozen had joined them and another five lingered in the hall.

Perhaps the woman wouldn't come because Rosa was there, outside and on the porch, in clear view of the garden. From somewhere distant, the call of a whippoorwill sounded, but it wasn't close enough to be an omen of anything at the house. At some other house, perhaps, someone was about to die. What must that be like, knowing you would close your eyes one final time and never see, hear, or feel anything again? Did you carry the taste of your last meal to the other side? Did you really pass through a billowing white veil? Was it cold, when your blood stopped flowing?

She opened the knife to test the thought. Over the whisper white scars she'd already drawn, she cut a thin line in her arm. A sliver of blood rose there, silver in the moonlight, beautiful and enthralling. The liquid felt warm and thick, as if it had been a substantial part of her. Maybe there was a limit to how much blood a person could spill before they ceased to be. She squeezed her fist to tighten her biceps and force a tiny droplet of blood to seep out. The pain was warm, not hot. The cold air stole that warmth. Rosa closed the knife and returned it to her pocket. The raven had moved closer and made a sound not unlike the whippoorwill's. And a woman walked through the rose garden.

She was paler than Rosa had imagined, and certainly unreal. Walking among the roses with her hands out to her sides, feeling the petals and the thorns, the woman reminded Rosa of herself as a child first walking among the roses.

The woman paused, turned to look at her, and smiled a real, genuine smile.

In that moment, Rosa saw the details of her face. The eyes were too close together, crowding her nose; and her ears were not quite symmetrical. There was no color, only pale ash, so much softer and lighter a shade than the gray of the uncles Rosa was tempted to call it white. But it was actually the color of the moonlight, as though the substance of the woman was merely reflections in the mist. Her lips had a suggestion of pink, their vibrancy muted. Her eyes revealed only a tint of amber, the same as the wolves, the same as the uncles, the same as Rosa herself and her mother.

The woman walked the length of the garden, and there plucked one of the roses. She looked again at Rosa, then stepped out of the garden and into the field.

Rosa climbed out of her chair and followed.

Mist drifted across the fields, obscuring any sight of the woods. The woman seemed almost to glow. Rosa followed, not hurrying, merely matching the woman's pace. The raven followed at a distance or from a height, seeming to keep within an eye's distance, coming closer as the mists thickened.

Mist swallowed the house behind Rosa.

Without meaning to, Rosa closed the distance between her and the woman, maybe because the fog thickened, maybe because the woman slowed as they neared the edge of the forest. Here, a small stream wound into the fields from the forest and curled back into the trees. Rosa had never noticed it before. But this wasn't her part of the forest. She normally ventured in other directions, where wolves stood watch over the gravestones.

The woman stopped beside the stream where it broke free of the trees. She looked at Rosa, beckoning her forward, then down into the little gully. That it existed at all was something of a surprise. The raven alit in the trees at the edge of the forest. Rosa looked into the water.

She saw dirt and roots and the thinnest stream of water. There were rocks, but there was also something shiny, something unnatural, the type of thing the raven would bring as a gift.

Rosa climbed into the muddy stream. She reached into the water to retrieve a thin silver chain. It was wound within a rock, so Rosa had to dig through the dirt to get it out. But it was no rock she dug around. It was a skull. A human skull smoothed by the water, a skull that had been buried in the dirt and unearthed by the stream.

When Rosa looked up to the woman, she had vanished.

Rosa washed the skull in the stream, which was hardly sufficient. She held up the chain to offer it to the raven. The bird came, plucked it from her hand, and flew off, disappearing in the night as she often did. The rest of the skeleton must have been elsewhere, or buried too deeply.

Rosa took the skull back to the house.

The field seemed uneven, with exposed roots trying to trip her up. The weeds, normally bending to the wind, writhing with life, reaching out in front of her to bar her path. But Rosa knew the way back to her own house, even if she couldn't see it. The forest had not tried to swallow her, so the fields would be unable to deter her.

Wolfsong rose in the distance, but they weren't a threat. Clouds finally hid the moon entirely, but that left only the house to light her way. Wil-o'-the-wisps, fairies, fireflies, whatever else might try to trick her in the distance, couldn't compete. A distant flicker of lightning only inspired her to hurry. She didn't want to get caught in a deluge. Her mother would kill her, or would maybe lock her out of the house, and she couldn't be sure the watchmaker would let her in from his side of it.

She saw the rose garden first. One of the uncles sat on the stone bench. He didn't look in her direction, merely stared at one of the demi-statues, a goddess with snakes in her hair and more coiled around her feet. The statue seemed almost alive in the waning light of the moon, and she practically danced in the flickering of approaching lightning.

Rosa stopped to stare at the uncle. He seemed sad, forlorn, maybe even lost. He looked down at his feet, at his open palms resting on his knees, then up at the statue's face as if imploring it for answers. Rosa was moved. How could she not be? She said, "Are you okay, uncle?"

The uncle turned to look at her. His cheeks glistened wetly in the last of the night's light. Then, in another flicker of lightning, she saw the skull beneath his skin and too many teeth.

The color in his eyes seemed to intensify as he rose to his feet.

Rosa's heart skipped a beat. Her breath caught in her throat. The uncle came toward her, fists at his sides, with immense speed. He opened his mouth to say something, but stopped when he saw the skull in her hands.

The uncle stopped, stared at it, and with his mouth already open, screamed.

The scream started high and loud, and rose from there, increasing in intensity and in pitch, scratching against the insides of Rosa's ears and brain. The forest trees trembled. The house rumbled. Thunder vibrated in the sky and let fall all the rain. He had been about to attack or consume her, but now the uncle cried to all the heavens and all the hells, disturbing ghosts in their crypts and disquieting the wolves who responded with howls of their own from all directions.

Rosa stepped away and screamed, "Stop!" But the uncle wouldn't. The scream only grew louder. She ran to the house, up the porch steps and inside. She threw shut the door behind her, and only then did the scream stop.

The foyer was empty. The halls were empty. When she ran past the parlor, she saw her mother slumped over in the chair next to the hearth, a glass of wine on the table beside her. Was she asleep or dead? Now wasn't the time to check. She raced upstairs, seeing no one and nothing, and into her rooms. She locked the door. She threw herself on her bed, buried her head under the pillow, tried to drown out the memories and echoes of that scream. She got blood on her sheets, not from the slice in her arm but from her ears, both of which leaked.

She didn't care. Face buried, panting, she waited until her heart was calmed enough to move again. Every vein inside her pulsed with the activity. That scream had been awful and otherworldly.

Eventually, she climbed out of bed. She brought the skull into her bathroom and set it on the shelf nearest the tub. She wanted her pocket watch, to rub the etched raven's face with her thumb, to garner some sense of safety from it. She settled for the crystalized rose, fragile and delicate as it may be. Her blood, frozen with the dew into those black petals, vibrated in sympathy with her racing pulse.

As she calmed, she examined the skull, the cavities of its eyes and nose, the rows of chomping teeth, the smooth cap and the crack that ran halfway up from one of the earholes. She turned it over in her hands, feeling its weight, understanding its frailty. She smoothed the head as though there were hair there. She said, "I'll take care of you, don't worry."

The skull gave no response. But someone knocked on her bedroom window.

The raven had returned. She carried something, but it was not the silver chain. Rosa opened the window. The bird dropped the flower and flew away.

It was a rose.

A black rose.

It was the rose the woman had picked in the garden before leading Rosa to the skull.

She stared at it a while, almost afraid to touch it. Somehow, it belonged with the skull. Both skull and rose had probably belonged to the same woman. The stem was short, but long enough to stick through an earhole. It took some propping to get it to stand upright and not sag to one side or the other. In this way, the skull looked like it wore a dying black rose in its hair.

The skull said nothing, merely stared at her, accused her, pitied her, shamed her. Rosa turned it around so the skull wouldn't look at her in the bathroom or in her bed. Instead, it stared into the corner of the room, where there was no one and nothing, not even spiders, not even shadows.

Rosa did not sleep soundly. She spent most the night on top of her bed staring at the ceiling. There were no secrets there, no constellations, nothing. She had ruined her sheets with rainwater and blood. The storm raged all night outside. She sought comfort in the displays of lightning, the booms of thunder. At one point, she heard footsteps outside her room – only her mother made such sounds when she walked through the house. Her mother stopped out there, touched the knob – it rattled gently – then went away with an audible sigh.

Rosa squeezed her eyes shut then. She drifted, once or twice, waking to a violent volley of thunder cracks or the scratching of fingernails against her door or the sound of her doorknob rattling.

Then she woke and found her bedroom door wide open. The window was open, the curtains dancing wildly in the wind, rain pouring in with incessant lightning. Shadows streaked across her room, the walls and floor and ceiling. Uncles had crowded through her open door, three or four of them there either staring at her or at the window, another two standing outside her closet.

They weren't supposed to be able to get in. Her mother had the only other key. The uncles had never – except that one time, and only one of them then – been in her room. It was hers, and hers alone, a private and personal sanctuary.

She flew out of bed like a whirlwind. She shooed the uncles at her doorway back into the hall. She screamed at the uncles outside her closet – and another three inside, she actually swung at, as though her little fists carried strength enough to threaten grown men. Inside her bathroom, three of them gathered about the shattered skull. It had come down and splintered on the tile floor. The petals of the black rose were strewn among the bone shards. The uncles gave the pieces a respectful space. When she picked up one of the bigger pieces, a fractured section of the jaw, they backed away from her.

She wielded it like a weapon. "Out!"

They retreated out of the bathroom, then out of her rooms. Her mother stood at the door, attracted like a moth to the noise. The uncles broke around her as though she were a boulder in the midst of a river.

Rosa, still panting, still holding the jawbone like a blade, looked at her mother.

Her mother touched her chest, a pendant she wore around her neck. Her robe fell open enough to reveal there was nothing else there, where she usually carried the second key to Rosa's room on a chain. Her eyes went wide. "They took it."

Rosa stepped forward. "What?"

"One of your uncles," her mother said, her voice barely a whisper as she realized what had happened. "I kept it close, but..." She shuddered. Then she turned her attention to the state of the room. "Close that window, girl. And look at your bed. What a mess."

"What a mess?" Rosa asked, stepping forward again. "There were *uncles* in my rooms."

Her mother shook her head. "It won't happen again, I can assure you of that."

"But you can't," Rosa said. "Where's the key?"

The key was gone. Her mother ignored the question. "Clean up in here, and don't come out again until it's spotless, you understand?"

Rosa slammed the door shut. Her mother was close enough, Rosa risked slamming it into her face, but she didn't care. She locked the door with her key, the only one she had, knowing it would only keep her mother out now.

She went to the window and let the rain pummel her and the

wind tangle her hair. It had gone pale again anyway. She watched the lightning and the forest and the vegetable garden and the wolves she couldn't see and everything else in the world. She wanted to be anywhere else.

When she cleaned up her rooms, she gathered and kept the bone shards in another box in her closet. The crystal rose hadn't been touched. The feather. Even the knife remained untouched. If they had come because of the skull, maybe she should keep it somewhere else. But where in the house could she hide the pieces that the uncles wouldn't find them?

She couldn't hide them anywhere inside her house, but maybe in the other house.

She didn't try to sleep after that. In the morning, in the storm, she went outside and found the watchmaker's door to the basement. It was an old, maybe ancient space, and the nature of its mushrooms and fungi had changed. She found a crevice in the stone walls where the skull might have fit perfectly. It barely held the box, so instead she emptied it, piling the bones and the rose petals in a kind of monument. She kept the piece of the jawbone as a form of security. She wondered if the watchmaker would approve. She hoped the woman would. Or the raven.

CLOCKWORK RAVENS

13.

Winter came harshly. Storm after storm caused the house to shudder. The uncles seemed preoccupied, which was good, and Rosa had taken to pushing a table in front of her door every night. It was a heavy table. And though the uncles could probably push the door open anyway, there was no way anyone would be able to sneak in, day or night.

One night, Rosa heard the piano.

One night, Rosa watched the rose garden from the porch until the cold drove her inside.

Snow covered the fields and covered the forest, burying the gardens. The wolves prowled closer to the house, though she only saw them at or near night. They circled it like predators because they were predators, and Rosa began to wonder if they considered her or the uncles prey.

When finally the days started to get longer again, the storms came more swiftly and violently. She heard the cracks of falling trees in the forest. She saw no trace of the raven after it had brought her the rose.

But then, one night, something tapped at her window.

It was still winter. It was most certainly a raven, but not her raven. Not the one who brought her gifts. She opened the window and saw that it was, in fact, not a raven, but a facsimile of one, a mechanical bird with black metallic feathers and a glassy black eye. She heard the gears inside it. It clicked, more like a lock or a clock than like the raven, then flew away. It circled over the vegetable garden, then crossed over the house directly above Rosa's rooms.

She ran to the other side of the house, to the sitting room with a view of the mound of snow that hid the rose garden, but saw no sign of the clockwork bird.

It was the watchmaker's, of course. He had shown her the plans, and had finally succeeded at creating something that could fly. Was it a success? Did it have any purpose other than to make her smile? Because it succeeded at that. She smiled, and she kept the smile for most the day, so that even at the supper table her mother asked, "What is the matter with you?"

"Nothing," Rosa lied. "Nothing at all."

One night, from her window, Rosa saw the big wolf looking up at her. His fur hid him in the snowy night, but his eyes glimmered. While he seemed to be alone, she knew the other wolves must have lurked in the shadows. It was sometime after midnight, and she'd awakened for no apparent reason, so she pulled on something warm to venture outside.

The slivered moon reflected off the windblown snow. She had to cover part of her face because the dancing snow carried tiny ice shards. The wolf hadn't gone. When she stepped off the porch, he only moved his head to keep his eyes on her.

She took a breath before continuing. The vegetable garden was invisible except for a slight mound in the snow.

Was the wolf trying to warn her of something, or merely luring her outside because he was hungry? As she got closer, the wolf's eyes betrayed nothing but warmth and sorrow; but when he smiled, he bared powerful, seemingly inevitable teeth. The moon also smiled, but without the implied menace.

As she came closer, the wolf lowered his head to look more directly at her. Those eyes felt like weighted spears driving through her head and her heart. She came within ten feet of the wolf. Striking distance. If the rest of his pack laid in wait, now would be their opportunity. She glanced left and right but caught no sign of movement.

"You aren't so bad, are you?" she asked.

The wolf growled.

His fur bristled, his haunches tightened, his teeth grew in prominence. But Rosa did not back down. She withdrew her knife, opened it, revealing its blade. She wasn't unarmed. The wolf, however, seemed unimpressed. He took a deliberate step forward, then another, halving the distance between them.

Rosa held her breath. She kept her eyes locked on the wolf's. If this was meant to be a show of dominance, she had one other weapon. She withdrew the shard of jawbone, the only part of the skull she hadn't buried under the house. She brandished it like a weapon. She grinned. And from somewhere deep inside her, someplace she maybe didn't know she had, Rosa growled.

This made the wolf pause.

Wind whipped snow around in little whirlwinds. Otherwise, the night was still, virtually silent, and the two of them faced each other under the spotlight of the moon. The wolf seemed to walk on the snow, which made him taller than Rosa, knee deep. The cold might defeat her. It seeped under her skin, through her bones and veins. But she refused to back down. The wolf needed to know who she was and what she was capable of.

She didn't even know that.

She took one step forward. The snow resisted, the wind kicked up, the moon seemed to blink – and the wolf lowered his head and gave a little whimper.

It was a small sound, and it didn't last long, but it was a sign of submission. A moment later, he turned and ran. He fled the house in a straight line across the fields until he disappeared into the forest.

Finally, Rosa allowed herself to breathe, to gasp a lungful of air at a time. Her grips, on knife and bone, whitened her knuckles.

The next day, she dyed her hair the darkest, deepest red yet. She used a mixture of crushed berries and the reddest roses, both having been drying in her closet since before winter, and several drops of blood to create one color. Then she used fresh roses, red and pink and as dark as the garden offered, for the complimentary color. They both looked like dark shades of red. She streaked them through her hair in clumps, intermingling them, and loved the initial result. When she went to the dining table, the uncles noticed, and they seemed to take a step back from her.

The color didn't last. It never did. By the next day, it was already starting to fade. But as it faded every day, it changed, making her something of a chameleon who could disguise herself in the sunlight. The moon, merely reflecting sunlight, granted her a mystical stealth. She took to going out at midnight, racing through the snow around the house, over the vegetable garden and rose garden, finding she could tread over the snow as easily as the wolf when she put her mind to it.

She slept later in the day. She had to guess as to the exact time, but her body sensed the transition from one day to the next. She never saw the wolf, but heard his song in the distance. She saw no other creatures, either. They kept clear of her. Eventually, after days and weeks, she ran as far as the edge of the forest.

She wouldn't enter the forest. Not at night. It was another world inside, and there was no guarantee she'd ever find her way home again. The string she'd tied years ago might be a good guide, but there was only one string and a thousand trees. She felt powerful in the snow, in the cold, a red streak because she moved with supernatural speed. She was strongest in this winter.

She stopped, one night, at the edge of the stream. It had hardly left the forest. She searched for other bones, but never found any. Either the stream had swallowed them, or it had only carried the skull out of the forest.

A few nights later, she followed the stream into the forest. It would guide her back out again when she needed to escape.

The winter brush was less a wall than during the summer. When she passed into the forest, she entered another world. The limbs of trees were like skinless arms. Knots in the trunks resembled faces. The shadows were thicker and stronger, a miasma that slowed her progress. She didn't just walk near the stream, but took to wading through it. The water was slight and shallow, and in some places solid ice, so she didn't get too wet avoiding the viscous forest night. There was less snow under the trees, splashes of it where there might have been moss, and no moonlight.

In the dark, the forest sang. It was a dangerous song, though, filled with the rhythms of creatures moving, twigs snapping, crisp leaves crackling underfoot. Once, she spied something – or thought she did – massive, ten times her size, with a head full of antlers like an array of spears. Those spikes dripped with blood. She hunkered low in the stream's gully, which really wasn't deep, and held her breath as it passed. It breathed fire, or at least exhaled plumes of white smoke. Either it didn't notice her, which seemed unlikely, or it didn't care. The wolves, the whole pack of them, might be able to bring this creature down, but not if a single one of them was weak or tired that night.

There were other sounds, distant sounds, violins and guitars, unidentifiable instruments surely played by dark wintry fairies. If they found her, they would catch her, they would flay the skin from her bones, they would keep her alive suspended in a cage.

The stream wound through the forest without destination. A

fear grew inside her: that the stream would shift behind her and never lead her out of the forest again. She might wait until dawn and use the light to her advantage – unless she had somehow crossed a boundary into a place where the sun never rose.

She never found more bones.

Up ahead, she saw fire, she heard voices. She crouched low as she approached, though she didn't want to. She didn't know how far from home she'd strayed. She spied on the camp, three or five men in tents, a bonfire, laughter and axes and rifles.

She had never seen anyone else before, not in all of her memory. Even these men were obscured shapes distorted by the dancing flames. They looked demonic, more substantial than the uncles but also darker. Whereas the uncles were gray, these men were shadows brought to life. They thrilled but also frightened her. They spoke music, a language unlike hers or the watchmaker's. They weren't supposed to be here. They, too, had ventured far from home.

Her heart raced as she spied on them. She wondered if the pocket watch, which undoubtedly had run to its end by now, would have mimicked her quickened heartbeat. She didn't get too close. She didn't break a twig or touch a dry leaf. They were drinking and laughing and telling stories, and maybe they shouldn't have heard her anyhow.

Then, all at once, all their heads turned in her direction. There were seven of them visible now, as though the night had multiplied them, and they had heard something.

Rosa fled.

She fled quietly and slowly down the stream. She looked over her shoulder several times. They were calling to each other, pacing her, not caring that they'd startled her, probably carrying those rifles and big knives.

It was a long flight. She never saw them, but heard their

laughter, their feet, their heartbeats. But even the seven of them together couldn't match her pace as she broke free of the forest.

Her house was barely visible against the horizon. The moon gave the field light, but the snow reflected every moonbeam. When they emerged from the forest, they would see her; and even if they didn't, there was no place to run but the house.

She ran anyway. With all her speed, all her strength, every ounce of every breath. She didn't look back until she was more than halfway to the house. They were chasing her, wading through the snow, spread out in a long line. There were more than seven. She'd never had trouble counting before. Their numbers seemed to fluctuate. Something about them was wrong, wicked, even evil.

One of them spotted her, yelled to his companions, pointed at her with his long rifle – and a thunderous boom cracked the night.

It was a sound she knew. She'd always thought it was axes against trees, but it had always been the gunfire of hunters.

Closer to the house, near the rose garden, Rosa tripped and fell. She crashed through the snow. It swallowed her. Rose vines entangled her under the snow. She ripped through some. Thorns bit into her. And one of the uncles emerged onto the porch.

Rosa stopped struggling.

Not one uncle. Three. Seven. Twenty.

They carried no weapons, but they stared out over the field at the approaching hunters. Even Rosa's mother emerged from the house, wrapping herself tightly within her robe. Her face was flushed, her breaths unsteady. Rosa resisted calling out to her. The uncles moved.

Her mother remained on the porch.

The uncles charged into the night just as the one had against the wolves. This time, they outnumbered the threat. In the snow, in the moonlight, with tremendous speed, they moved invisibly. When they reached the hunters, they severed heads, disarmed the hunters at the shoulder, sprayed their blood like rain in the snowy fields.

Like Rosa's, the uncles' feet made no impression in the snow.

Just a few breaths later, there was nothing left of the hunters. The uncles walked back to the house, slowly and deliberately, without a word and without a sound. Even the moon seemed to recede from them. They tread across the snow and returned towards the house like soldiers from war.

Rosa's mother retreated into the house.

Rosa waited in the rose garden, where the thorns had dug into her skin like claws, where the vines had tangled her legs and wrists like ropes. Snow and penetrating ice snuck in through her pores. She shivered, and she wiped away a frozen tear, and she watched as the nearest of the uncles passed by looking down at her with a gray, ghastly grin.

When they were all inside, when the night had gone deathly still once again, Rosa disentangled herself from the rose vines. She bled from a dozen cuts and scrapes. She shivered. She trembled. Her heart had slowed, but was still twice its normal pace. She felt the thrum of blood in her throat, her arms, her thighs, behind her eyes.

She was a mess, soaked by the snow, frozen by her own sweat, not sure if she was excited or frightened. She walked quietly to the porch, up the steps, and into the house. She half expected her mother to be waiting there. Instead, she heard sobs from within the house, rhythmic and pained. Slowly, at the end of her strength, Rosa climbed the stairs and made her way to her room.

The door was open.

The door should not have been open.

Inside, one of the uncles sat in her chair. He grinned at her. He held a key in his blood-stained hand. His fingernails had been the blades that cut the hunters' flesh. His teeth were like those of the wolf. He said her name. He said it once, rolling the R, his eyes focused so intently on her, the heat of them cut through her skull. That heat did nothing to ease the cold that had burrowed into her.

"That's my key," she said. "You're not supposed to be in here."

He shook his head. His grin spread. The number of teeth in his grin grew. He shrugged. "It is *my* key, Rosa." Then he repeated words he'd said to her before: "*You owe me your life.*"

She approached him. She still shivered from the cold, but he must have mistook that for fear. She withdrew the jawbone from a pocket in her dress. It wasn't large, but it was warm, warmer even than the air in the house. The uncle's eyes fell on the bone. His grin wavered, but he did not move. He said, "Child."

She said, "Uncle."

Then she stabbed him. Quickly. She got the shoulder. She had never tried to stab someone before. It plunged into his ashen flesh, tearing through his suit, and drew blood. Bright red blood, vibrant blood, shimmering blood.

He moved then.

He exploded from the chair, pushing her aside, ripping free of the jawbone. She managed to keep her hold on it. It ripped more of his flesh as he fled. Out of the room, out through the door, down the hall and down the stairs. She didn't care to know where he went. She shut the door. Locked it. Pushed the heavy table in front of it.

She bent over the blood that had spilled redly on the floor. As it dried, it seemed to shift to silver. The blood made a shape on the floor, like a snake or dragon, and it was incredibly beautiful. Some teeth had broken loose from the jawbone and fallen in a similar pattern on the rug.

She wouldn't clean that blood. Let it stain. Let it become part of her room. Let it stand as a warning to the other uncles: she was prepared to fight, and she was dangerous.

She pulled the blankets from her bed and slept, on the floor, curled in much the same shape as the line of silvery red blood. When she woke, still gripping the jawbone, the light of day bright through the window, the color of the blood had shifted to black. But when she looked carefully, when she got down on the floor and put her eye practically in the fibers of the rug, she saw traces of silver and traces of red.

It hadn't been a dream. She had made one of the uncles bleed.

Outside, the snow had started to melt. Winter had officially come to an end.

Over the next few days, the snow melted away entirely. The nights were getting shorter. She'd stopped running through them, not sure there was anything more to discover. She locked herself mostly in her rooms. She'd trembled for three days after the incident with the hunters, and didn't see her mother at all in that time. She took the hottest baths she could stand, and drew the cold from her veins with short incisions.

One day, she went to the sitting room. The only snow she could see anymore was well beyond the rose garden, and all of that had been stained red.

When she went to the dining table for breakfast, her mother's eyes were pale, bloodshot, and rimmed with black. She looked at Rosa and frowned and didn't prepare a plate. Rosa had to get her own. It was the first time, but it seemed natural. They ate in silence. It was there that Rosa noticed the scars on her mother's wrists and the yellowish bruises around her throat. The uncles seemed absent that morning. It would have been a good time to talk. There was probably much that needed to be said, but they weren't about to start now.

The uncles had gathered in the parlor. As she passed it, Rosa couldn't get an idea of which she had stabbed with the jawbone. They had always been interchangeable, but now one of them was marked, even if the wound was under his suit, hidden by jacket and shirt, obscured by the gray. She watched for a while from the hallway. They seemed to ignore her, mostly, but threw glances in her direction as if she might not notice. They spoke in hushes whispers. They might have talked textiles, opera, and baseball. They might have talked about their victory against the hunters in the field. Maybe they would write songs about how they had defended the house, Rosa, and her mother from the lascivious designs of wicked hunters. Maybe they congratulated each other.

Maybe the wolves would have come to defend Rosa.

And maybe Rosa had never needed defending in the first place.

Days later, the raven returned.

CLOCKWORK RAVENS

14.

It was still too cold to leave the windows open, so the raven knocked. She looked smaller than usual, and the sheen in her feathers had faded some. She came into the room, perched on her desk, and dropped a gift.

At first, Rosa thought it was another pocket watch, copper or bronze in color, but there was no casing to open and the face was composed of two crossed lines, one marked with the letter N, and a floating arrow that spun as she moved it. A compass. An old compass, dirt-smudged and blood-stained. The glass above the face was cracked in a spider-web pattern which disturbed the movement of the arrow.

"Thank you," she said to the raven. She turned it around so that the arrow would show her north. But it wasn't right. It was off by at least forty-five degrees.

Once upon a time, she suspected, it had belonged to one of the hunters. Maybe then, in the forest, it had pointed true. But now, it showed east, something just shy of east, as north. It pointed toward – and beyond – the rose garden.

It was the same size and weight as the pocket watch. She missed that. It had been made into something beautiful. She wondered if the watchmaker could repair the compass, too. She wondered if she would just lose it in the forest, or in the fields, or to one of the uncles.

"How was your winter?" she asked the raven.

The raven cooed. It was a caw, but it sounded warmer, more personal, more honest. She smiled at the bird, laid her head on the desk next to her, and said, "I think I understand."

The raven fluttered her feathers, clicked a few times, then flew out the window again. She flew over the top of the house, toward the rose garden.

Rosa ran to the sitting room on the opposite side of the house. It took a minute to pick out the raven perched on the arm of one of the statues. The garden was primarily vines and bushes, with only a few blooms sticking out.

The watchmaker was already out there with his basket and shears. He was clipping the heads of black roses. In the past, there had only ever been one, maybe two at a time. Now, he seemed to stop frequently, shaking his head, cutting at least four or five, crushing those petals and dropping them into his basket.

Maybe she should use the black petals to dye her hair next time.

She didn't want to call to him from the window of the sitting room. Besides not speaking the same language, she didn't want to attract the attention of the uncles. Or her mother. She ran downstairs and outside to the garden as the watchmaker was making his way back to his secret door.

"Hi," she said, out of breath, when she reached him.

He said the same, or something similar, in his own language.

"What happens to those?" she asked, pointing to the basket. He had cut at least seven black roses.

He lifted the basket and looked into it, then back at Rosa. He said something she didn't understand and shook his head. She got the meaning. He wasn't going to give her the flowers.

"Please." It wasn't exactly a plea. She didn't know how to do that. But she needed the flowers, and the only other way to get them was to wait for more black roses to bloom.

He didn't respond. He went through the door. He closed it

behind him. She waited, counted to ten even, then opened the door.

He wasn't there. It was just the wide, long basement. She wove through the patches of mushrooms until she got to the small alcove with the skull fragments. She took a breath. Among the broken bones were the dried, desiccated petals of a single black rose. She'd already used some in the past. She gathered the rest, stuffed them into a pocket, and fled the basement. It was cold and musty and unpleasant today – it was every time, actually, just more noticeably now – and she didn't want to get stuck there. There was always the risk of some aggressive fungus overextending its reach and trapping her.

Outside again, she didn't have to look behind her to confirm the door disappeared. She walked instead to the rose garden, to the bench nearest the raven, and sat for a while. She didn't focus her thoughts on anything in particular, and instead looked around the garden to see if the watchmaker had missed anything. If there had been seven black roses, then maybe there had been an eighth or even a ninth.

She found one. Only one. It was small, barely open, but thoroughly black from its outer edge to its heart. She pulled it out of the bush without shears. The raven cried out, but only briefly. She looked at the bird, asking if she was wrong, but the raven offered no response. She merely remained there, sitting, peering, dreaming corvidaen dreams, seeing things undreamt by Rosa. "Lenore," she said, voicing the raven's name she'd hardly ever used since the day she'd offered it. "Where do you fly to when winter comes?"

The raven offered neither hint nor whisper of a response.

"Maybe it's best I don't know," Rosa said, pulling the compass out of her pocket, wondering if it would lead her to the raven's wintry hideaway. That season was at an end. The raven's return made that explicit. There were many months before she would make that flight again. Maybe, in that time, Rosa would gather the courage to follow her.

That didn't prevent her from wandering. A week or two later, in the weak light of dawn, Rosa set out in the direction the compass pointed. She didn't bother trying to sneak around her mother anymore; the older woman seemed too busy, too absent to notice. The uncles followed her progress through the house, and sometimes stood at windows when she was outside. She knew now they could follow her, could stalk her and even hunt her when she went into the woods. She went armed with the broken jawbone and her knife.

The compass led her *north*, which was closer to east, so the sun was bright against her eyes for the first part of her walk. She went past the rose garden but not quite in the direction of the stream or where the hunters had been slaughtered. She didn't forget that they'd intended to kill or catch her. But it was vital that she remembered the relentlessness of the uncles, their silent efficacy, their trek back to the house as though they'd been soldiers.

Eventually, Rosa reached the edge of the woods. She marked her entry with another string. She hadn't had to do that in a long time. It was a bright piece of string so it would be easy to find if she had to escape in a hurry. She no longer trusted the woods, not entirely.

Inside, the trees were just beginning to green again, so the canopy above her was broken, letting fall long, thin shafts of sunlight. She stepped around these, afraid they might be dangerous in ways she couldn't imagine. The light was harsh, and the lusciousness of the forest was still struggling to reemerge.

She followed deer paths for a while, but remained ever

straight, guided by the compass, seeking out whatever secrets the raven had intended for her to find.

She found a tree trunk with a face carved into it. She examined its features carefully: a nose, two eyes, a mouth opened into an O. But it was wrong to say it had been *carved*; these shapes were natural. They'd probably been there longer than she'd been alive. The sentinel watched for the approach of anyone or anything – Rosa inclusive – and somehow, perhaps through its roots, reported back.

"I mean no harm," Rosa told the trunk. It was just a trunk, cut off about ten feet above the ground, so that the rest of the tree had long since disappeared. Even still, there was growth, tiny limbs sprouting the barest of leaves struggling to linger in the thin line of sunlight that struck it from above. The trunk gave no indication it heard her. She got close to the eyes, which were a little too high for her to look directly into, even on her tiptoes. They were almond shaped, complete with stubby irises. She didn't touch them. She knew how she'd feel if spiders crawled over her while she slept and started prodding at her eyes.

Deeper into the forest, the trees grew thicker, birds flew higher, small creatures like squirrels scattered. The sound of flowing water increased as the day grew longer, and eventually that sound was overcome by a crashing of water.

After some hours of walking, she came to a lake.

She had read about lakes, and seen illustrations in some of the books in her library, but she had never actually seen one. The lake wasn't as big as the house, but it was larger than the rose garden, and all sorts of vines and bushes and trees curled around its edges. The water itself was thick and dark. She could see the bottom of the lake only along the edge nearest her, where rocks and twigs and mud were inches below the surface.

The crashing of water came from the far side of the lake, where a creek spilled into it from a higher elevation. Cranes, foxes, deer, raccoons, and other creatures she didn't know gathered at the shores of the lake. She saw colorful snakes and salamanders and rabbits and bears.

At the lake, the compass ceased working. The needle no longer pointed a straight line, but spun lazily and erratically. This lake was its destination.

The animals, all of them, each in turn, took a moment to regard her, to assess her level of threat or potential as a meal. She felt incredibly small, even compared to mice and chipmunks. She felt unreal here, in a place so very solid and tangible. She knelt beside the lake, dipped her hand in. The water was cold. The animals coming to the lake seemed to drink and leave. She watched them for a while, seeing that pattern repeated by creatures of all sizes.

And it worked in the opposite direction. Small fish darted up against the edges of the lake. Larger fish loomed in the shadows. She couldn't see far into the water because it wasn't something she'd ever seen before. Shapes drifted under the water. Briefly, there was a struggle somewhere to her left, between something in the water and something at the water.

This wasn't a safe sanctuary.

But she wasn't about the ignore the apparent ceremony. She cupped her hand, drew water from the lake, and swallowed some. It was fresh, and blazed an icy trail down her throat. It invigorated her, if only briefly. She felt alive.

She wondered if the water was transformative. Would feathers slip from her pores on her walk back to the house? Would her nose blacken and grow solid and sharp so that she might feed on carrion in the fields? Would she bring gifts to a girl secluded in a faraway house?

She turned back the way she came. Beyond sight of the lake, the compass started working again, pointing behind her. She went the opposite direction of the arrow, though she realized no matter what direction she moved from the lake, the arrow would have pointed behind her. It wasn't trustworthy. So she had to rely on her own sense of direction, and her memories of the forest. Her feet knew the way, surely.

She passed the trunk. Its expression seemed to have changed, but it was hard to define. Was it softer or harder? She looked into the eye again. "Thank you," she said to the trunk, though she wasn't sure what she was thanking it for.

She found her string and emerged from the forest near twilight, so she again had to walk toward the sun. She put the compass in her box in the closet. At the supper table, her mother asked, "Where do you go?"

"What do you mean?" Rosa asked. "There is nowhere to go."

"You know what I mean."

She didn't really. But looking at her mother, Rosa saw her eyes were sallow, the skin there puffy, and there were more visible bruises on her arm and neck.

"You're bruised," Rosa said.

Her mother put her fork down. She was about to launch into a tirade, and took a deep inhalation to start, but she let it go with a defeated sigh. "I am."

"Why?"

"I bump into things at night," her mother said. "I didn't use to bruise so easily."

"Bump into things?"

"I sleepwalk."

"I've never seen it," Rosa said.

"I walk in other places," her mother said, retrieving her fork. "Now eat, before it gets cold."

Rosa said nothing more. She ate. She thought about the other places her mother might be walking. Could there be another house, not just the watchmaker's, within these walls? A third house? But that would be too much, wouldn't it? Already, the dimensions confused her. She had counted windows outside and in, she had counted doors, she had made sketches and kept them tied together with the red ribbon the raven had once brought her. She'd tried to include the little she knew about the other house, and it simply didn't fit.

"What's in the basement?" Rosa asked suddenly.

Her mother stopped eating, the fork halfway to her mouth. She looked across the table, across her forkful of food, but never answered. Instead, she resumed eating as though the question had merely been a curtain fluttering in the wind.

One of the uncles said, quite succinctly, without otherwise seeming to acknowledge Rosa or her mother, "There is no basement."

Then he left the room. The other uncles in the dining room continued as they were, stealing quick glances in Rosa's direction.

After that, she saw her mother less and less. Her mother didn't come to meals, didn't berate her about anything, didn't watch her in the rose garden, nothing.

The uncles acted more erratically, wandering halls, stopping to stare at paintings sometimes but also at the wallpaper, as though those repeated patterns revealed secrets of the world. For her birthday, Rosa's mother came to the parlor, not to the dining room, and set a record into the player. She had grown pale and jaundiced, resembling a yellowish version of the uncles. She sat in the chair by the hearth, played the record, but refused to dance. When she coughed, there was blood.

The uncles were agitated, anxious and active, for weeks

afterwards. Finally, early one morning a few months later, a knock on Rosa's door woke her. She had to push the table out of the way of the door to answer it. She found seven uncles standing there. They all looked down and away, anywhere but at her. One of them said, "Your presence is required."

In her nightclothes, Rosa followed them to her mother's rooms. They were on the other side of the house, in a suite of small rooms, one big room with a massive bed draped in gossamer and silk, and one bathroom. Rosa didn't remember ever coming to her mother's rooms before. There were paintings on the walls, life-sized statues on the floor, a shelf full of books and knickknacks. Those surprised Rosa. She wanted to examine them, but that would have to wait for another time. They reminded her of the gifts the raven had brought to her.

In the middle of the bed, sunken into cushions and pillows and sheets, attended by the uncles, her mother's eyes were open but she wasn't seeing anything – nothing there, anyhow. Maybe she saw other worlds, other hallways in the house, other uncles, even her husband – Rosa's father – who had died before they ever came to be in this house.

Rosa knew he'd existed, but remembered nothing else.

She didn't even know if the uncles were from her father's side of the family or her mother's.

Her mother looked through eyes that could not possibly see anything in this room or this house. They were clouded over, obviously unfocused, distant and lost. She moved her lips, muttering, sounding like the uncles when they were being quiet. Suddenly, she turned her head from one side to the other and flailed her arms. "Rosa!" she called, her voice barely more than a whisper.

Rosa caught her mother's hand. "I'm here."

"Rosa," she said, intentionally whispering, so lightly that Rosa had to lean closer to hear. "Are we alone?"

"There are the uncles," Rosa said.

Her mother lowered her voice more. She spoke straight into Rosa's ear, maybe straight into the brain. She said, "Don't trust them."

Those were her final words. A minute later, her mother exhaled and never inhaled. She stopped moving. The unfocused eyes lost all semblance of life. The last trace of amber in them vanished completely.

Rosa didn't release her mother's hand.

The uncles wept. The sound of their weeping swept through the halls of the house, every floor, every alcove and crevice, every hidden room she had never uncovered.

One of the uncles banged a fist on the big mirror in her mother's bedroom. It didn't crack or even shake, but it sounded like something had shattered. Another uncle wailed. One put his hands on Rosa's shoulders as an act of consolation.

But Rosa didn't feel sad.

She didn't feel happy, either. She felt empty. As though a part of her had vanished. It didn't make sense, so she didn't try to make sense of it. She tried to draw a breath but found it difficult. She forced it anyhow, and it got caught in her throat.

One of the uncles opened the window.

A raven arrived. The uncles retreated from it. Rosa looked, and saw it was not Lenore. This bird was smaller, rounder, sharper, more vibrant in his black feathers. Of course, there had always been two of them, hadn't there? Ravens took partners for life. They'd probably had a hundred little ravens over the years, all flying off in different directions, finding other girls and women to befriend, other souls to comfort.

The raven flew from the windowsill to the foot of the bed. The uncles closed the doors so he couldn't fly freely around the house, but otherwise gave him a lot of room.

The raven cawed and clicked, then landed on her mother's chest. He scratched one talonned foot there. He said something, an honest word, in a language Rosa didn't know. She stared. The raven fluttered his wings, lifted off her dead mother's sheets, and flew out the window.

The room felt colder after that. The uncles closed the window and latched it tight.

Rosa wandered, eventually reaching the dining room. She was the woman of the house now. She was alone. She had always been alone, but not physically, not utterly, not to this degree. She wandered the halls without aim, stopped downstairs when she reached the dining room, and fried some eggs in the skillet. She knew she needed to eat, but they were tasteless, not because of how she felt but because she hadn't added enough salt. She tried another batch, and this time used too much salt, enough to scare away snails and slugs. She retreated to the rose garden and sat the rest of the day on the stone bench, staring sightlessly at the goddesses and queens. If they invited her now to fairy dance halls, she might not have noticed. She didn't realize how cold it had gotten until the sun settled behind the forest. She didn't see the wolves, standing in formation right at the edge of the trees, until they started howling. All of them. All at once. A symphony – or a cacophony, she wasn't sure.

Inside the house, she asked one of the uncles, "Where are the records?"

There were about fifty, in all, stacked on a shelf in her mother's rooms. They had covers she had never seen, emerald or gold or black, with names of the artists and songs. She carried all of these to the parlor, set them near the record player, and started playing them.

All night, past midnight, through dawn and beyond, Rosa

played all the records, every one. She had never heard most of them. One was only a saxophone, another a harp. There were orchestras and quartets and singers with voices that must've come straight from the fairy dance halls. She had never heard singing like that. Those were songs her mother could never have brought out.

The uncles came and went. Some lingered in the parlor, perhaps listening, sometimes just watching her. They were open about it now, staring and leering, barely restraining themselves. They whispered amongst each other, but even if they hadn't been keeping their voices secretive she would not have heard them. She heard the music, and followed the strains of it to other worlds, even if only inside her mind.

The uncles carried her mother out past the vegetable garden to the house graveyard. Rosa went with them as they buried her. Clouds hung low on the horizon. Other stones bore names Rosa didn't recognize. Some matches the names of authors found in the library. One matched the name signed on the bottom of at least a few of the house's paintings. Other uncles crowded around the grave as the pallbearers lowered the corpse into the ground. Her stone had already been prepared.

It seemed like every uncle turned out. For a brief moment, the house was empty and unprotected. The wolves broke out in a new round of howling as the body was lowered. Two ravens perched on other stones in the graveyard.

How had she never seen these stones before? It was like a garden of granite, no bigger than the rose garden on the other side of the house but certainly no smaller. There were little statues, icons, rings of flowers and mushrooms, ribbons, even a rolled up scroll that had been leaning against the face of one of the stones so long it had started to disintegrate. Lilies had grown up around another as if preparing to pull it into the ground. The name had been scratched out of one stone, though the date of death remained.

Did these stones tell her family's history? She knew none of these names, not even her mother's, not really. She walked away from the burial before they were done, back to the house. One of the ravens, Lenore, flew with her, hers, and landed on her shoulder. That was new. She smiled. She whispered, "Everything will be alright, right?"

The raven clicked – a no, Rosa thought – and flew away, dropping a feather. Another feather. This wasn't the first time. Rosa caught it before it reached the ground. It shimmered with traces of blue and indigo, like the feather once lost in the snow, but also red, like Rosa's hair sometimes.

She locked herself in her room after that. She prepared another batch of dye, the darkest she'd ever made, shattering the black crystal rose and grinding its shards into dust, using the petals she had gathered, and washed oblivion into her white hair. At first, the color merely smeared and streaked, but with some work and effort, with some sweat, she drove that shimmering darkness into the hearts of every strand of hair on her head. She got reds and blacks in ways she had only ever imagined before. It was rich, thick, and extraordinary. When she slept, she stained her pillows and sheets crimson. She was okay with that. It reminded her of blood. In the silvery light of the moon, it was like her bed had become an endless abyss. She had never slept so well or so thoroughly.

On the third night, the uncles started knocking on her door.

That first knock was light, three almost reluctant little sounds. One of the uncles said through the door, "You have to eat."

It was true. But she didn't want to. She had water, and rose petals, the last few bars of chocolate in her stash, and whatever the raven brought her. But the raven didn't bring food.

Through the night, uncles paced outside her door. She heard them shuffling over the carpet. She heard them stopping at the door. In the morning, after the raven never arrived with food, her stomach rumbled and she felt too weak to move the table out of the way. But she did so.

The uncles stood back as she pulled open the door.

She stepped into the hall, locked the door, slipped the key into her pocket and gripped the broken jawbone she would now have to with her at all times. It had proven effective once. She wasn't sure what the uncles wanted from her, but she didn't want to give it to them.

For the moment, they seemed to only want her to eat. A feast had been prepared: three kinds of vegetables from the garden, fresh bread, spiced meat, red wine. She ate too eagerly, with gusto, to fill her tiny but hollow stomach. The uncles stood back, approving of her appetite, offering butter for the bread, taking dishes as she emptied them, refilling her wine glass.

It felt like all the uncles watched her eat. There were hundreds, surely, an infinite supply of uncles, grayed faces with amber flecks in their eyes, neat suits, spindly limbs. Some wore spectacles; their eyes seemed oversized and oversaturated. Others carried books. Ledgers. Fountain pens.

Finally, when Rosa felt like she couldn't eat another mouthful, the plates before her were cleared and an assortment of pies laid out on the table: blueberry, cherry, apple, chocolate.

When one of the uncles laid the last of the pies – apricot and almond – she looked up at him as if to ask why. He smiled sadly. He said, "We eat in honor of the recently departed."

She sampled all the pies. She drank too much wine. It swirled in her head. She usually only drank a glass; tonight, she think she finished a whole bottle. When she was done, when she pushed away the last dish and said, "I can't," she had to hold on to the table to stand. But before she made it three steps, music burst out of the parlor.

"To honor all lost souls," one of the uncles said, "we dance."

It was a song Rosa recognized. The minor keys. The melody. The shifts in intention. It was the watchmaker's song. Instead of just a piano, there was a whole orchestra. The flutes handled a particularly delicate part. When it got violent and frantic, there were trumpets and horns and a deep, frantic bass struggling to hold the other instruments in time.

The uncles all wanted to dance. She danced with them, one after the other, just a few steps with each before being passed on to the next. Her head swam. She didn't feel safe, but she felt warm. When the song ended, one of the uncles reset the needle and started it again. In such a manner, they danced, swayed, swam through the lightheadedness of the wine.

One after the other, they held her, danced with her, guided her through the motions; they held her up, supported her, refused to let her drop.

Rosa was tired.

But there were still more uncles. They weren't all the same. Some were taller, thinner, straighter, rougher. Some wore single breasted jackets instead of double breasted. A few had bowties. One had a monocle on a chain. Some had mustaches. Some seemed too young for that. They held her closer, tighter, stronger, and as the night progressed the music changed and the dancing became more frenetic, more frantic, more frivolous.

She didn't feel frivolity in any part of her, especially not her heart. She tried to push away from one dancer, but the uncle resisted. When he passed her to someone else, she realized she was nothing more than a ragdoll tossed amongst dogs.

"Stop," she said at some point. Begged. Pleaded. Demanded.

One of the uncles reset the needle and the record started again.

"No!" she cried, finally pulling free of the uncle's grip. Backing away from him, she realized she was surrounded by the uncles, dozens of them, a thick mob of uncles who weren't about to let her go. All their eyes together didn't have as much amber as her own – or her mother's, but her mother was dead and there was no one left to protect her.

She withdrew the jawbone and commanded, "Back!"

They eyed the weapon with some respect, but they weren't about to be chased away. She was theirs, and by becoming the woman of the house, she had assumed certain responsibilities they wouldn't let her shun.

She thrust the jawbone at the nearest of the uncles. He backed away. That was good; it meant the bone could hurt them. She slashed it in the air in front of her, sliced and hacked. She was barely able to keep her feet. Had the uncles laced the food with something? Was she under their spell? Was it merely the wine? The hollowness inside her?

She forced herself forward, into the hall, away from the music and the dancing, away from the uncles. They made disappointed chittering sounds as they paced her up the stairs, following her on all sides, staying only arm's length away to avoid taking a swipe of bone in the gut.

She made the landing, ran crookedly down the hall, cheered and jeered by the uncles behind her. They didn't follow her. They let her run to her room. On the other side of the door, she locked it again, then shoved the table into place, using what must be the last of her strength to do so.

Panting, heaving, she fell to her knees, dropped the jawbone, and cried.

"You owe me your life."

One of the uncles, one whom she'd previously stabbed with the jawbone, who favored his shoulder because of the wound, stood inside her room. He still possessed the other key. He could come and go at will. He hadn't been one of her dance partners in the parlor. He'd been waiting for her here, in her chair and by her window, in her room.

He'd been waiting, and had continued to wait as she locked herself in with him.

The amber in the uncle's eyes gleamed.

He loomed over her. In the dark of night, he seemed to be twice her height, towering over her, bending at the middle to look down on her. He grinned. She scrambled for the jawbone, but he kicked it aside and under the bed.

He stepped closer. She crawled backward, but immediately ran into the table blocking the door. He stepped closer again.

She pulled the knife from her pocket. Opened it. Thrust up at the uncle's chest. She hit him in the stomach; from that low angle, she drove it straight up, behind the ribs and sternum, into his heart. She hadn't realized the blade was long enough to do that, or that she had strength enough.

The uncle seemed surprised. His mouth echoed the O of the tree in the forest. His eyes went wide, wider than they've ever been, and all the color drained from them as he looked down at her. His blood, however, was brilliant red, brighter than her hair ever had been or could be, richer than the sun at its fiery sunset, more vibrant even than her own blood in the moonlight.

He fell to one knee. He stared at her. He said, "You *dare?*" If there was more to the question, he never got it out. Those were his final words. He pulled the blade from his chest, ripping more of his flesh, splitting and spoiling his suit, gasping with the pain of it. With a last surge of strength, he lunged at her with the blade.

He missed. Or she successfully avoided him. Or the blade itself deflected his assault. She couldn't be sure. He fell, face down, on the carpet in front of him, on the stains of his own blood. She had wounded him before, and now she'd slain him. He twitched a moment, then went perfectly still. She couldn't recall noticing if the uncles had drawn breath, but this uncle, at least, had ceased. Blood oozed out from under him. Rosa climbed into her bed, wrapped her arms around her knees, and watched as her uncle failed to move, failed to stand, and eventually failed to bleed anymore.

Uncles congregated outside her door.

Rosa merely breathed, and stared, and wondered what would happen next. Another burial? Another feast? Would they feast on her?

At the window, the raven knocked one last time. She opened the window, and the raven hopped in, shivering despite that winter was gone. The raven cawed once, then scratched its talon along the desk to leave one final gift behind: a slash in the wood.

Ravens weren't eternal. They didn't live forever. No matter what Plutonian shore had been her home, she wouldn't be returning. Lenore fell over, spilling one final black feather. Like the others, the color wasn't entire and complete; a sheen of red, of bloody crimson, ran along its razor edge.

Rosa stroked the feather. She lay her head on the desk and touched the raven. A tear spilled wetly and heavily from her eye and dropped on the desk. The wood absorbed it immediately. In that way, a part of her would remain at this house forever. But she could not. The uncles would demand retribution. They might merely kill her, but she couldn't hope for that. They would punish her. They would cause her great pain, suffering, humiliation. She might never see the outside again. No forest, no rode garden, not even her mother's grave.

She looked out the window. Storm clouds were moving in. Thunder rumbled from such a distance, she hadn't heard it through the glass. The wind was picking up, but there was no sign of rain yet. If she'd still had her pocket watch, she might confirm it was past midnight.

She couldn't stay in the house anymore.

She took her compass. She didn't know what else she would need. She changed into her special dress, the one in which she'd most recently sewn the button and the diamond earring and the bottle cap. She slipped into her best, most comfortable shoes. She checked herself in the mirror. Her hair was a black and red storm, all askew and misaligned. Her face was red. She splashed herself two, three times. She checked her teeth. Briefly, she examined her fingernails. She picked up the broken jawbone and put it in a pocket. Then she crawled under the bed, all the way, to retrieve the knife. She felt most at risk then, as though the dead uncle might suddenly raise its head and catch her by the ankle before she could wriggle away.

Instead, the uncles outside her door knocked.

When she didn't answer the knock, it turned into pounding.

She climbed out the window. She dangled. It had never seemed like so far a drop. She held her breath, closed her eyes, and let go.

She tumbled forever. It was an endless drop, ending in soft earth and grass. Her legs bent. She tumbled backwards. Nothing hurt, nothing serious. She walked around the back of the house. The forest glowed in the dark. Forest sounds reached her: the howling of wolves.

She passed through the rose garden. She didn't stop. There was no time for stopping. "Goodbye," she said to the statues as she passed. "Goodbye, and thank you."

The statues didn't respond.

Uncles, however, emerged from the house. First, they were on the porch. Rosa put the garden behind her, and the uncles entered the field. A hundred of them, maybe a thousand. They had always been impossible to count, especially in the dark, especially with the mist floating so low to the ground tonight. The moon offered some light, but barely enough to read the compass.

She walked until she felt the need to run, but her ankles – the left one, in particular – wouldn't hold her that long. She must've twisted something in her drop. She tried to ignore it, tried to press on, tried to run but could only maintain half her usual speed.

When she looked back, the uncles seemed iridescent in the moonlight. They came after her in a long, horizontal line, so that there seemed to be nowhere to run left or right. They were faster than she was. They were angry. They murmured, chittered, whispered.

There was a good chance she'd never reach the forest. And even if she did, all she heard ahead of her was the howling of wolves.

15.

Maybe her ankle had hurt from the moment she dropped from the window. But every step made it worse, hotter and more intense, broader in reach and scope. Halfway across the field, halfway to the wall of the forest that didn't even promise salvation, she lost her footing and fell.

She looked back. The uncles were coming, and they were close. They moved swiftly and silently, a line cutting through the night. She scrambled to her feet again and continued to run. They shouldn't be able to catch her. They seemed to not move with any hurry. But their faces were contortions of anger and fury. She focused on the line in the trees.

The wolves stopped howling.

Two dozen of them waited at the edge of the forest. They watched with amber eyes. She didn't understand her relationship with the uncles and the wolves, but only the raven – and maybe the watchmaker, she'd never noticed – had eyes of any other color.

They exuded patience. They watched her run toward them. They seemed hungry, in the way that wolves were always hungry. They seemed formidable. And they seemed preferable to the uncles.

But finally, she lost the strength of will to run. Halfway between the wolves and the uncles, under the silvery light of the moon, she stopped running and turned to accept her fate. She couldn't run headlong into claws and teeth, but she could stand and face whatever the uncles delivered.

The big wolf, whom she'd met twice alone, let out a single bark, and the wolves sprang toward her. They were fast, faster even than the uncles. They overtook her and kept going. They met the uncles and attacked.

The uncles defended themselves.

Rosa took a breath and began again to run.

She broke into the forest and was instantly enveloped by a cool darkness. The moon barely penetrated the canopy. She took a moment to look back, to see the wolves and the uncles slashing and gnawing at each other. They fought almost soundlessly. None of the uncles broke through the line of wolves.

Briefly, she checked the compass, and followed the arrow.

The forest was different in the dark, thicker and more ominous, filled with sounds other than wolfsong: the rending of flesh, the flight of prey; the crashing of things too large for the forest paths; and whispers among the trees and shadows, unintelligible words in a language not meant for human mouths or ears.

She had to move slower in the woods than her ankle demanded because of the brambles, the roots snaking in and out of the trees, and the possibility of predators bigger even than wolves.

No paths guided her to where she was going. She didn't really know. The compass led only to the lake. Breathlessly, favoring her ankle, she worked her way deeper into the forest. The tree limbs crowded her and grabbed at her hair, dark as the forest night. She'd stopped looking back. It would only disorient her. Either she was a creature of the forest and other creatures would defend her, or the uncles would never come beyond the tree line anyway. The knife and jawbone would not be enough to fend them off.

Sometime later, some hours or days or years, Rosa reached the trunk. Its expression had changed again. Its mouth had closed, its eyes narrowed. It seemed angry and threatening, but not toward her. She said, "Thank you."

Not long later, Rosa heard the waterfall and saw the lake. It shimmered in the moonlight. Only then did she look back.

She saw the line of uncles behind her, and not far behind her. They were searching. They couldn't see her like she could see them. She couldn't run anymore. She was out of breath. Her ankle burned and threatened to shatter under the demands she'd made of it. Rosa slipped silently into the lake, a few meters beyond the shore, where it went quickly from shallow to deep. She felt fish caressing her legs and torso as she moved into the water. They weren't all as small as what she'd ever seen at the shore.

The uncles reached the lake and stopped.

They sniffed. They closed ranks close to the water. Some bled. The wolves had done damage. Ultimately, there had been too many uncles for the wolves to hold back.

The water came up to her chest. She didn't dare go out farther. She crouched, so that the water covered all but her face. If they saw her, she'd risk the lake, she'd swim for the waterfall. She didn't know how to swim, but need would propel her.

The uncles looked about the clearing by the lake. They muttered and clicked and made inhuman sounds she had never heard them make. They were still tall and thin, but somehow appeared more animalistic outside of the house. She didn't wish them dead, merely gone. She didn't understand how she was related to them, or how she had lived under their roof for so long.

They seemed unwilling to leave. The trail they'd been following – her scent – had led here but no further. She lowered herself in the water. Only her nose and eyes remained above the surface. And her hair, which floated on the water, and bled out its dyes, black on the ebon surface. It reflected none of the moonlight, but inevitably would reveal her.

Something long snaked around her calf under the water.

Rosa held her ground.

Then the uncles did something that surprised her. They started to cry. Not all of them at once: first one, then another, then a third leaned against one of the trees, wailing and kicking its trunk. Something dropped from the tree and hit the uncle's head.

They looked much the same as they had in her mother's room when she'd died.

And eventually, they started back toward the house. Away from the lake. They moved slowly, dejectedly. One, maybe, looked out toward the middle of the lake, but he didn't seem to notice her. He was the last of the uncles to leave.

Rosa waited a long time after that, never certain they had gone far.

The cold water seeped through her skin the whole time. Ruined her hair and ruined her dress and, presumably, ruined her. She shivered under the water, and eventually climbed back to the shore. Laying there on her back, staring up at the silvery moon through the break in the trees, her heavy breaths became gradually shallow. She wanted to close her eyes, to sleep and perchance dream, but that promised no relief. If the uncles returned, or the wolves were still hungry, or something else stumbled upon her on the edge of the lake, she would be unable to defend herself.

She heard a sound like a watch, like her watch, the pocket watch she had lost in the field when the uncle defended her from the wolves. She wondered now how that might have gone differently if she hadn't run. She opened her eyes – she didn't remember closing them, only thinking about it – and saw a raven beside her, a metallic black raven with eyes like crystal and a beak like a pair of blades.

It regarded her a moment. She nodded, accepting whatever fate it would deliver.

The clockwork raven pecked at her shoulder. Like a needle stick, the pain was beautiful and reminded her she was alive. The raven pecked her again, this time drawing a thin strip of her flesh away and flying off with it.

Another mechanical raven pecked at her waist, piercing her dress and flesh. A spot of blood spread silvery from the wound it made. Rosa sighed. It was lovely, a lovely way to die, a gift, far better than wasting away under the command of the uncles.

A third bird pulled a string of her flesh from her shoulder. Exquisite pain ran down her nervous system. Another bit of flesh was taken from her thigh. Her wrist. Her cheek.

The clockwork ravens were quick about their work. There was a lot of her to take away, one silver blood drop, one sliver of skin, one strand of hair at a time. She reached up, the last of her strength, to caress one. It struck her finger. The blood reminded her of beauty, of grace, of love – things she maybe knew nothing about, but she was reminded, nonetheless.

Somewhere in the sky above, the moon had slipped to the farthest edge of sight, and the sun had broken an unseen horizon. Stars disappeared, one at a time, with the lightening of the night. The moon slid slowly past the trees. The ravens peeled away pieces of Rosa, and she welcomed it, welcomed the little pains, the blood, and reminders that she had, indeed, been alive.

They continued to work even after she closed her eyes, and took those as well.

16.

Rosa hadn't expected to wake. She felt pinpricks of pain throughout her body, over her skin but also her muscles, even in her bones. But already the pains were fading. They were memories of another life, perhaps. She wasn't sure.

She opened her eyes, but she was covered. Not by sheets, not by silk, but by dirt and brittle leaves. How long had she been asleep? She pushed herself up. It was a struggle, but she'd been buried at the surface, not deep, not so she would suffocate in the earth.

She reached for the sky, and something banged in her hand. The compass on a chain? No: the pocket watch was tangled in her fingers.

Rosa reached a sitting position. Blinking, she looked around. This wasn't the lake. It was the graveyard, the little hidden graveyard in the forest. She counted only five stones. There had been a dozen the first time, and fewer every time she came. She read the names on the stone, the lettering no longer a mystery to her, and recognized some of them. Was that her mother's name? She didn't know. The stone she woke in front of had her name, or the name of an ancestor she'd never known. This made her smile. She wiped her mouth, spitting out the detritus of the forest.

A clockwork raven buzzed and chirped on the gravestone beside her. It didn't sound like her raven and barely looked like her raven. It carried something small and shiny in its metal talon. When she reached out with her hand cupped, the bird dropped the key into her hand.

Her muscles were stiff. The daylight, even filtered in the forest, hurt her eyes. Eventually, she realized she only had one choice now. She couldn't live in the forest. There were no other choices. She had to go back to the house. Maybe enough time had passed that the uncles had abandoned it. She could lock herself in her rooms. Or maybe this key would give her access to other rooms where the uncles would never find her. Maybe she could have her own entrance and exit into the house, and she could co-exist with the uncles so long as she kept herself primarily invisible.

Her body was covered with the scars of reassembly. The clockwork ravens had brought her here, piece by piece, and she smiled at the thought.

When she rose, the raven beside her fluttered its metallic wings. She used the stone to support herself. She was weak, tired, and hungry. She was dirty to the core, and possibly beneath the skin.

Rosa made her way slowly through the forest. She leaned on the trees more than she should have. She reached the string she had tied to a tree years ago. She pulled it loose. It came away easily. She crawled out of the forest.

The field was awfully bright. The rose garden gleamed in the distance. She trudged slowly to the house, careful to maintain her balance. Her dress was a tattered mess, no longer white at all but the reddish brown of her dried blood.

Strangely, she felt alive. Every beat of her heart was like a hammer driving her forward. Every tentative step through the field gave her strength enough for the next. The clockwork raven soared above her, swooping low every so often, joined by its friends. She counted seven, though there might have been more.

She paused a few times, simply standing in the field to regain her breath. When she was close enough, she saw someone sitting in the rose garden. She thought it might have been her mother, but he was broader and taller than her mother, and older, his skin more like leather, and he wore his familiar purple coat. He turned to watch her approach. She didn't go straight to the house.

She sat in the rose garden beside the watchmaker. She leaned her head on his shoulder and, briefly, cried. He put an arm around her shoulders like a father might. She had never known her father, not really. He had died before they came to the house, but she remembered nothing from before the house. She had lost a whole lifetime somewhere. She mourned what she'd never known.

"All will be okay," the watchmaker said to her, patting her shoulder.

She said, "I know." Either she spoke his language, or he spoke hers. She didn't waste time trying to figure it out.

He led her into the house, but the hallways were not the halls she knew. The rooms were different, and in different places. He took her first to the dining room, which was smaller and unoccupied. He brought her bread and wine. He brought her a small piece of meat. "Slow," he said, so she ate slowly, and drank only half the wine before asking for water.

Upstairs, he led her to her rooms, which were exactly where they had been. He gestured to the lock. The key, not her old key but the one brought to her by the raven, unlocked the door. He said goodnight, and closed the door behind him.

They were her rooms, just as they'd always been. There was no corpse of an uncle, a new rug to replace what had been stained by his blood and life, and fresh silk sheets on the bed. In the bathroom mirror, her hair glistened whitely, despite the dirt and muck caught there. She'd been scarred across her face as well as her arms. She ran a bath, and found scars all over her body as she climbed into the hot water.

She hadn't felt warmth or heat in so very long; she had no means of counting the time.

She lived now in the house within her house. If she snuck through a half-door, or out into the garden, and found one of the uncles, he might recognize her, but they would no longer share a language.

The heat of the bath reinvigorated her some. She slept soundly that night, and perhaps for days, but she woke hungry and found a feast awaiting her in the dining room: pancakes and biscuits, bacon and sausage, heaping piles of blueberries and strawberries, even a tall glass of fresh chocolate milk.

"Is it my birthday?" she asked the watchmaker.

"We can pretend it is," he said.

They ate in silence. Over the next few days, she explored the house. Except for her rooms, they were different; they'd been folded to take the spaces between rooms of the other house. Here, her rooms somehow faced the rose garden. Over the next few days, she went out to the roses and its statues, but she always eyed the house carefully. What if it shimmered and became her old house? What if the uncles found her?

She went, too, to the vegetable garden, and to the family graveyard, to her mother's stone. She couldn't read the letters. Her mother's name faded completely from her memory.

Sometimes, when she passed one of the big mirrors in the hall, she saw uncles on the other side. They roamed the halls listlessly, hanging their heads, sometimes crying or wailing – but she never heard them. One time, an uncle saw her through the glass, and sprang at her, shattering the mirror on the other side. Here, she only saw the cracks briefly, a spreading spider web that faded entirely.

Eventually, the watchmaker showed her the rooms in which he tinkered. He'd made thirteen of the clockwork ravens, and had to wind them each morning if they were to fly with autonomy. He had a collection of watches and clocks and little figurines which represented a family he said once lived in this house. "Long ago," he said, "and far away."

"What happened?" she asked.

He shook his head sadly. "I don't know."

He kept his secrets. That was okay. He smiled often, though he moved slowly – he had gotten very old, older than anyone Rosa had ever seen – so that his skin wrinkled, and his lips cracked – but his eyes never faded from their vibrant amber – the same as Rosa's eyes, which had never quite been the same as her mother's, and never the same as the wolves', and never the same as the uncles' eyes.

ACKNOWLEDGEMENTS

First and most importantly, I must thank Morgan for being the kind of friend I needed when I most needed one, for walking (and dancing) with me through the darkness, and without whom none of this would have been possible.

Inspirational research for this project focused on Edgar Allan Poe's "The Raven," especially readings by Basil Rathbone and Christopher Lee; Oscar Wide's "The Nightingale and the Rose;" Hans Christian Andersen's "The Nightingale;" and Guillermo del Toro's *Pan's Labyrinth*, as well as many late night conversations and dreamings with my dark fae.

I have to thank Brent for giving me a space to do that research, and my sister and her husband, Jeneine and Chuck, for giving me a space to write this.

As always, a special thanks to Sabine and the Rose Fairy.

ABOUT THE AUTHOR

John Urbancik has often dreamt of clockworks in various guises.

In addition to books of poetry and photography, and a nonfiction book based on the 100 episode run of his podcast *Inkstains* (in turn based on his three-time year-long projects of the same name), Urbancik (pronounced Urban as in City, Sick as in Puppy) has written books like the *DarkWalker* series, *Stale Reality* (also available in Russian), *Choose Your Doom*, *The Night Carnival*, and *The Secret History of the Palace Theater*.

Born on a small island in the northeast United States called Manhattan, he is currently sequestered in an undisclosed location in the woods of Pennsylvania near the Susquehanna River.

www.DarkFluidity.com

ALSO BY JOHN URBANCIK

COLLECTIONS
Shadows, Legends & Secrets
Sound and Vision
Tales of the Fantastic and the Phantasmagoric
The Museum of Curiosities

POETRY
John the Revelator
Odyssey
Annabel Lee, in Shadow

NOVELLAS
A Game of Colors
The Rise and Fall of Babylon (with Brian Keene)
Wings of the Butterfly
House of Shadow and Ash
Necropolis
Quicksilver
Beneath Midnight
Zombies vs. Aliens vs. Robots vs. Cowboys vs.
Ninja vs. Investment Bankers vs. Green Berets
Colette and the Tiger
Madmen, Poets & Thieves
Clockwork Ravens
The Night Carnival
La Casa del Diablo

ALSO BY JOHN URBANCIK

NOVELS
Sins of Blood and Stone
Breath of the Moon
Once Upon a Time in Midnight
Stale Reality
The Corpse and the Girl from Miami
DarkWalker 1: Hunting Grounds
DarkWalker 2: Inferno
DarkWalker 3: The Deep City
DarkWalker 4: Armageddon
DarkWalker 5: Ghost Stories
DarkWalker 6: Other Realms
Choose Your Doom
The Secret History of the Palace Theater

NONFICTION
InkStained: On Creativity, Writing, and Art

INKSTAINS
Multiple volumes

www.ingramcontent.com/pod-product-compliance
Lightning Source LLC
Chambersburg PA
CBHW051303250626
47155CB00009B/3417